And Then She Was Gone

Editor: Talia Leduc

ISBN-13: 9781998775217

Give feedback on the book at:
lorhainneeckhart@hotmail.com

Twitter: @LEckhart
Facebook: AuthorLorhainneEckhart

Printed in the U.S.A

And Then She Was Gone

THE O'CONNELLS
BOOK TWELVE

LORHAINNE ECKHART

The O'Connells of Livingston, Montana, are not your typical family. Follow them on their journey to the dark and dangerous side of love in a series of romantic thrillers you won't want to miss. Raised by a single mother after their father's mysterious disappearance eighteen years ago, the six grown siblings live in a small town with all kinds of hidden secrets, lies, and deception. Much like the contemporary family romance series focusing on the Friessens, this romantic suspense series follows the lives of the O'Connell family as each of the siblings searches for love.

The O'Connells

The Neighbor
The Third Call
The Secret Husband
The Quiet Day
The Commitment, An O'Connell Novella
The Missing Father
The Hometown Hero
Justice
The Family Secret
The Fallen O'Connell
The Return of the O'Connells
And The She Was Gone
The Stalker
The O'Connell Family Christmas
The Girl Next Door
Broken Promises
The Gatekeeper
The Hunted

About this book

The moment Brady told his family he was engaged, his fiancée was nowhere to be found.

Six months ago, Brady's true love, Cassie Arnold, walked into his hometown and his life. Everything was perfect, including their plans for their upcoming wedding—but one night, when he came home, Cassie was gone.

How could she just vanish?

Brady turns to his sheriff brother, Marcus O'Connell, and is stunned by what he discovers. Not only is there no trace of her, but it's as if she never existed.

As they dig deeper into the days before Cassie vanished, Brady is stunned to learn of a series of mysterious phone calls, and he realizes his bride-to-be and her seemingly perfect smile were hiding dark secrets, including an unsolved murder at her family's cabin in a hometown he's never heard of.

Brady soon suspects that to find Cassie, he may also have to figure out what really happened the night of the murder—and why Cassie kept it all a secret.

CHAPTER

One

How was it possible that Brady had woken up one day and become part of something bigger, something that still didn't seem real?

It was his nineteenth birthday today, and he wasn't sure what to expect as he walked down the street with his hands shoved in his lightweight black down winter jacket. He took in the familiar sidewalk, one he'd walked a hundred times, and the heavy clouds in the darkening sky. The unusual cold predicted an early snow any day.

As he arrived at Marcus's two-storey craftsman, he looked across the street to Ryan's. The two brothers lived in a neighborhood where all the homes were similar. Welcoming light drifted out the living room window. He took a second to look around at the vehicles of his family, reminding himself they weren't strangers. Harold's new KIA, Tessa's older Buick, the sheriff's car his brother drove, and Charlotte's Subaru were all in the driveway.

He breathed out fog. It was cold tonight.

"Hey, birthday boy. What are you doing standing out there? Get your ass in here."

Brady hadn't expected Luke back yet, and although his older-model pickup was nowhere to be seen, there he was, standing in the open door, wearing blue jeans and a faded T-shirt. It seemed he'd packed on even more muscle. He held a beer, sporting the beginnings of a beard, and his shoulder-length hair was hanging loose. So he was letting it grow back out.

"I didn't know you were back," Brady said. And where had he been? No one else asked, but he always did.

"Just got here," Luke said. "You didn't think I'd miss your birthday, did you? Kind of expected you to still be at my mom's place, but you were gone. You walk over?"

Brady stepped up onto the porch, hearing laughter and voices inside. His ears were stinging from the cold. "I stopped for a haircut," he said, though he wished he hadn't. He only ever went to Iris's place to change these days, and he couldn't remember the last time he'd even slept there.

"Short and neat for your birthday, or is it a girl you're trying to impress?" Luke said. "Get in here before you let all the heat out." He ran his hand roughly over Brady's head.

As Brady stepped inside the warm house, he thought of the girl whose smile had him taking a second and third glance in the mirror to check how he looked and how he dressed. "It was time for a cut, you know—but I probably should've asked where not to go."

Luke leaned on the railing, his expression puzzled, eyebrows knit. Amused? He wasn't so sure, but he knew Luke was ready to listen, as always.

"Brady, it's about time you got here," Ryan called out with a smile from the kitchen, the place everyone gathered.

Brady pulled off his coat. Luke was still watching him

with that heavy, patient gaze. He knew Luke had many depths to him.

"So where, pray tell, did you go, and what happened? Give me the scoop." Luke tossed his coat behind him on a chair as Brady kicked off his sneakers, which had seen better days.

"That place across from the diner, at the edge of downtown."

"Not Clarissa's?"

The way his brother said it had him hesitating a second. "Blond, heavyset, cakes the makeup on?"

"That's her, the very same. Let me guess: She pumped you for all the dirt on my mom…"

There it was again, that uncomfortable feeling he'd had the moment he figured out she knew who he was and was getting too familiar with him.

"How'd you know that?" Brady said. "Yeah, she knew who I was and asked about every one of you, then gave me a blow by blow of your entire lives from her perspective, even though I didn't ask."

Then there was the moment the conversation had shifted to Raymond, when she'd said how sorry she was to hear he was dead, and he'd wanted her to hurry the hell up so he could get his ass out of that chair and leave the salon before he said something he knew he couldn't.

"That's why she gets her hair done the county over when she's here," Luke said. "But you look good—almost too pretty." Luke rubbed his hair again roughly, playfully, the way he did too many times, and then had them walking into the kitchen.

Marcus was holding Cameron, who had just started walking. His first birthday was only a month away, around the corner, another big celebration, he was sure. He had dark hair and the O'Connell blue eyes Brady didn't. He wondered if he'd ever feel the close bond that seemed to exist naturally between his other siblings.

"About time you got here, kid. Was about to send out a search party for you," Owen said as he walked over with an open beer and slipped it to him.

Brady stared at it for a second, not missing the twitch of Owen's lips, and he didn't hesitate any further before lifting it to his lips and taking a swallow. "Thanks," he said.

Ryan gave him a smile, and Suzanne rolled her eyes, whereas Marcus angled his head and just shook it. He wondered for a moment whether Marcus would take the beer from him.

"Just FYI, kid, this is a one-time pass," Marcus said, sounding much like his dad. "I'll pretend I'm not seeing it, but one beer only, understand?" He gave a pointed look to Owen.

Alison was keeping to the background, her hair hiked high in a ponytail, her eyes coated with smoky shadow. The auburn shirt she wore was cut low in a V. He only nodded before he had to pull his gaze away. The tension still lingered. He wondered if it always would.

"I see you got a haircut, cleaned yourself up," Ryan said, Jenny leaning against him. "Since dinner isn't ready, we should give you your birthday present early…" His eyes flickered with the sort of teasing his brothers seemed ready and willing to dish out more and more to him as of late.

He heard the back door and spotted Harold, his blond hair in the same cop cut he always wore. The barbecue was smoking out back, and he was wearing only a navy sweater.

"The barbecue is ready. You want me to throw the burgers on?" Harold said, then walked over to him. "Hey, kid, happy birthday. I see we're now encouraging underage drinking."

He knew Harold was teasing, and Suzanne only shook her head from where she was dumping a premade salad into a bowl. She wore a baseball shirt that accentuated her tall, lanky frame.

"He's nineteen, everyone," she said. "He's legal to drink somewhere. And remember when you were sixteen, Marcus and Ryan, what happened to Mom's bottle of vodka?"

There was silence for a second as Marcus slid his gaze to Suzanne. Another layer was being peeled back, another secret. He figured Marcus and Ryan had a bunch of exploits they'd never share.

Suzanne crumpled up the salad bag and tossed it into the recycling bin under the sink. "By the way, Karen texted. She and Jack are coming tonight. Maybe we should hold off on the birthday gifts until they get here?"

Marcus handed a fussing Cameron, who was rubbing his eyes, off to Charlotte. "No, this gift is just from the brothers," he said. "You and Karen can add your gift when she gets here. Come on, Brady."

Marcus had his hand on his shoulder and was steering him into the living room, directing him to Charlotte's rocking chair by the window, and everyone seemed to follow them. Charlotte had gone upstairs, carrying Cameron, whom he could hear crying now, and Eva and Alison had gone with her.

"You got me a gift?" Brady said.

Marcus rested his hands on the back of the sofa and looked over to him, whereas Luke took the easy chair, and Owen sat on the sofa across from him and rested a foot on the coffee table, dressed in the same blue jeans he'd worn at the job site and his usual five o'clock shadow, because shaving was something he did only every few days.

"Yes. Let's start with the fact that words matter,"

Marcus said. "You're nineteen, which puts you squarely in that age category I remember well, where you operate from hot emotion and say the first thing that comes to mind. Your mouth is and will be an issue and can land you in a ton of hot water, so learn to dial it back, way back, so you don't have to wish you could go back and say nothing instead. Think first before you say anything. That will save you from landing in a world of trouble with the kind of words that can't be taken back."

Brady just stared at him before looking over to Jenny and Ryan. The way she looked down on him, he wondered whether he had done or said something he shouldn't have. At the same time, he was still looking for the gift. Had they hidden it? He leaned forward and looked around Luke.

"Okay, fine," he said. "Watch what I say. Got it—but I'm pretty thoughtful, I think…" He lifted the beer and took another swallow, still not believing that Marcus was looking the other way and letting him drink.

"Be a damn good brother," Ryan cut in, gesturing toward him before crossing his arms.

Brady just blinked, wondering what this was. "Okay… check. I didn't think I was a terrible brother. Is there something specific you're getting at in a brotherly way that I've missed? Is this the buildup to the gift?"

Across from him, Owen was giving him everything with that heavy gaze. Tessa sat on the arm of the sofa beside him, her blond hair pulled up in soft, wavy curls that couldn't be tamed. "Your gift is advice from your brothers," Owen said, "so listen up. We're a family. Being the youngest, you didn't grow up with us, so you don't know how things work. You're getting a crash course since you've been with us for only almost a year. Family comes first. If you get a call that your brother has found himself arrested and is in jail, you bail him out, no questions asked. Right, Ryan and Marcus?"

Brady realized he was serious. "What! Wait, one of you got arrested?" he said.

Ryan lifted his beer and shook his head, but the expression on his face said everything. "Yeah, at seventeen. Good thing Mom isn't here. We never told her about it."

He wondered if his eyes bugged out.

Marcus was still leaning on the back of the sofa, shaking his head. Brady was seeing his brother, the sheriff, through completely different eyes these days. Maybe he was human after all. Meanwhile, from the way Suzanne stared, he was pretty sure this was the first she was hearing of the arrest, as well.

"You're serious!" she said. "Holy shit, I never had any idea. Does Karen know?"

Marcus shook his head and let out a rude noise. "No one was supposed to know about it. Remember to take it to your grave. Pretty sure those were your words, Owen."

"Hey, you're the one who had the brilliant idea of setting Brady straight on how we work as a family," Owen said. "At least I haven't shared all your secrets."

Marcus grimaced as he stood up and then pulled a hand over his face. "I sold the '72 Chevy I was rebuilding —I loved that car—to bail your ass out," he said, gesturing to Ryan.

Suzanne was still staring in horror, while Harold seemed amused. Luke and Owen were shaking their heads. It seemed Brady had no idea of the escapades that went on in this family, among his siblings, whom he was still getting to know.

"Yeah, but the only reason I landed in jail was because of you," Ryan said. "I was just the one who got caught holding the spray cans."

"Only because I'm faster," Marcus said. "I could never figure out why the charges suddenly went away. Guess now we know."

"Dad," Ryan said.

"Never got the bail money back, though."

Harold let out a laugh and shook his head as if this wasn't the first time he'd heard something along these lines. Brady wondered at times whether Harold understood the siblings better than he ever would.

"Dad did say he was watching," Suzanne said. "Do you suppose he made sure the charges were dropped and your bail money disappeared to teach you a lesson?"

He spotted headlights outside. Karen, maybe. He missed her, considering she and Jack were now in Missoula, which meant she could no longer stick her nose in every part of his business. He never thought he'd miss that.

"Maybe," Marcus said. "It's likely, since Dad seemed to know the details of what we were doing."

"And what, exactly, were you doing?" Suzanne asked. "You never really answered us, Marcus, when Dad brought it up last year, saying he'd been watching. He mentioned a string of robberies."

Marcus shifted his stance. Brady could see he was uncomfortable in the spotlight. Something seemed to pass between him and Ryan. They really did seem like partners in crime.

"Dad was right: I was a little shit," Marcus said. "But now I'm not. End of story. Let's move on, because this is about Brady."

"He broke into several stores," Owen cut in. "One was to steal the spray paint, and you lifted some parts for the Chevy, stole some camping gear…what else was it?"

Brady looked over to Ryan and then Marcus, who just

cleared his throat. Jenny smacked Ryan's chest, but her amused expression said this was no surprise to her.

"And you knew?" Suzanne said.

Owen made a face and shrugged. "Who do you think helped Marcus get the money for his car and went with him to the cop shop to get Ryan out? You forget how I had to keep an eye on all of you."

"Okay, we're getting off track here," Marcus said. "The point is, Brady, you get yourself in a jam, you call. You don't try to figure it out yourself. We all are your first call, and that makes you ours. If we call you for help in any way, it's no questions asked. You just show up."

Brady wasn't sure what to make of that. On the sofa, Tessa shook her head, and Owen lifted his gaze to her, resting his hand on her thigh.

"Fine, got it," Brady said. "So if I get myself arrested, I'll call you, but seriously, I'm not planning on it."

"That's good," Owen said. "Keep your nose clean, stay out of trouble—"

"And be a damn hard worker," Luke jumped in, cutting Owen off.

"When you believe in something, you stand up for it," Owen said. "You do right by your family, and you know who your family is. We have your back, and it goes both ways. You don't go off half-cocked alone, like Luke," he added, looking over to him.

Luke seemed to be quite comfortable, but he never really knew what his brother was thinking. Maybe he needed to take their advice and check in with Luke, who hadn't let on how he was since splitting with Rosemary. He really did hide what he was thinking.

"Hey," Luke said, gesturing with his beer and taking them all in. "We all need time alone sometimes, but know I'm one call away and always have been. No questions asked, ever. You know that, all of you. Lost count of the jams and scrapes I've found myself in, cleaning up after you all."

"If you're hurting, scared, screwed up, or confused about anything, you come here, to us," Marcus said. "You get stuck in your head at times, Brady, and you wear your heart on your sleeve. That's good sometimes, but others it isn't."

"And you always do your best," Owen said. "There's no shame in doing average hard work, the kind you're doing. You've got a trade under your belt now, and you're set. You finish the job, no complaints."

Brady was working for his brother now in his plumbing business, apprenticing, because he hadn't come up with a better option. That day almost a year ago, before Iris and his dad had left again, Owen had simply pulled up in his plumbing van and said, "Get in!"

"You never gave me a choice," Brady said. "I finished high school and thought of taking a few courses at college, but when I couldn't get in, you said I had to do something instead of sitting around, so you made me carry your tools and watch over your shoulder, crawl into holes, get dirty every day… Have I complained yet?"

Owen didn't seem impressed. His older brother didn't say much but seemed to always have his eye on him, telling him where to go, which job site to be at, and what to do. He wondered when he should start looking for something else, but what? He had no experience and had never worked before, because his dad had always moved him to some new city or state before he could get too comfortable.

"Well, you just make sure you don't start complaining," Owen said. "Anyway, when it comes to family, we stand beside each other, all of us, no questions asked until after."

He heard a car door outside.

Marcus went over to the window and glanced out. "Karen and Jack are here," he said before striding back over to the sofa and resting his hands on his hips, dragging his gaze over to Brady. "So I'll leave you with this, young man: I stand up for what I believe in because it matters to me. I screwed up a lot. I had a head full of steam, and, as Owen has pointed out too many times, I was hell on wheels. But I was proud of that when I was your age. I still cringe, thinking back on what I did and what I said, but I cleaned up my act and got my shit together after a lot of years. Even though I'm proud of being, as people say, just an average guy, I'm always there for my family first. I'm a damn good brother, husband, father. If you get in trouble, I'm your first call, because I'm there, standing beside you no matter what. All of us are." He walked around the sofa and rested his hand on his shoulder. "You may not have the same last name as us, Brady, but you are an O'Connell, so don't forget that."

He heard the door open, then his sister's voice.

Marcus was still staring down at him. "So why don't you tell us about this girl you've been seeing?" he said.

Brady wondered for a second whether he was being followed. "What?"

"That's another thing about us," Marcus said. "We know everything that's going on, and we're in everyone's business. You think we don't know about that cute waitress you make eyes at every day at the diner? You stop in almost every day for lunch and take her out, and you think word wouldn't come back to us? Yet we haven't met her, so I figured it was time to sit you down so you understand how things work here."

What the hell was he supposed to say? This was his family, and they obviously knew about Cassie, but there was something appealing about keeping his love life separate from the O'Connells. He realized they were all staring at him, waiting for him to say something as he fought the urge to squirm under their scrutiny.

"I see you're having some trouble, Brady, so let me help you out," Marcus said. "Are you messing around with her, or is it serious?"

There were times brother Marcus became sheriff Marcus, and he felt the cop staring down on him now.

"Can I plead the fifth?" he said, squeezing his beer.

Marcus took a step back and shook his head. "Nope. So let's say you bring her around tomorrow night so we can meet her."

He wondered what would happen if he said no. No one said a word, and Marcus didn't move.

"Fine," was all he said.

Marcus stepped back and gestured to Luke, who reached behind his chair and slid a wrapped box over to him, saying, "Your other gift, young man. Happy birthday."

As he reached for the box, all he could think was that he'd been pulled into the most unusual family. He glanced up to Alison, who was following Charlotte and Eva down the stairs. There she was, the reason he hadn't brought Cassie around and was still dancing in the shadows with her.

Awkwardness still lingered with Alison, but maybe Marcus was right. It was time to move on.

CHAPTER

Two

Brady rode shotgun in Owen's plumbing van, like he did every day, as they parked in front of Molly's Diner, taking the last spot on the busy street. It was lunchtime, and the diner was as busy as usual.

He spotted Cassie through the window, and it was the same every time: His heartbeat kicked up and time stood still.

"Okay, Romeo, go in and ask her, or are you going to sit out here and stare, all starry eyed?" Owen said. The van was no longer running, and Owen opened his door. He was going to follow him in, something he'd never done. Brady just stared at him for another second as Owen slid out, reaching for his dark blue hoodie, which had seen better days.

"I can't believe you're doing this," Brady said. "You know my love life is just that, mine. I'm feeling very much as if you're holding a gun to my head. I don't appreciate this." He pulled at the door and stepped out into the cool fall weather, but at least it wasn't as cold as last night.

"It's lunchtime. I'm hungry. What's the big deal?"

He realized his brother was taking tremendous joy from this, far too much, at his expense. "You never go in here—like, ever. But today you're dogging my heels."

Owen didn't even shrug. He pulled open the glass industrial door and gestured for Brady to go first. There it was again, Owen's ability to hide what he was thinking or feeling.

He stepped inside and took in the booths, all full except for one. Cassie was behind the counter, pouring coffee for a man who was smiling and staring at her breasts in a way that had Brady looking a little closer. He took a seat at one of three empty stools at the counter, and Owen sat beside him.

Cassie spotted him and gave him that smile, the one just for him. She started his way. "Hey, I didn't see you last night," she said, then turned to take in Owen. Her long dark wavy hair, which he loved running his fingers through, was pulled back. And then there was her smile.

"Yeah, sorry about that," he said. "It was late by the time I got home, and I didn't want to call and wake you." He felt a nudge, his brother's elbow in his side. "Uh, Cassie, this is my brother Owen." He cleared his throat.

Her smile widened. "Hey, I've heard a lot about you, Owen. Brady talks nonstop about you all. You two here for lunch?" She glanced between them, and there were those dimples, the first thing about her that had completely sucked him in.

"Yeah whatever the special is today," Brady said, but she started shaking her head.

"Liver and onions," she said. The way her eyes widened and she flattened her lips, he got her warning.

"Oh, good call," he said. "I'll have the cheeseburger with fries."

"Yeah, I'll take the liver," Owen said, leaning on the counter.

He didn't miss the shock on Cassie's face, and he turned to stare at Owen, who only shrugged.

"What can I say? I always liked it if it's cooked right. It's not something I can ever cook around Tessa. I suggested it once and even picked it up, but she said no, and in the garbage it went."

"Okay, one liver and onions and one cheeseburger," Cassie said. She reached for a cup and filled it with ice and water, then slid it in front of Brady. That was all he ever drank at the diner, likely because it didn't cost anything. "Owen, can I get you something to drink?"

Owen took in the water and gestured to it. "Water's good. Nice to meet you, Cassie." He nudged Brady, who lifted the glass of water and swallowed as Cassie put their orders in. "Come on, stop dancing around. She's cute."

Brady put his glass down just as Cassie settled one in front of Owen. "Hey, listen, Cassie," he said. "Just wanted to ask you if you wanted to meet the rest of my family. They were actually asking about you, so how about it?"

From the way Cassie was staring at him, he wasn't sure what she'd say, but she shrugged and laughed softly. "That sounds fun. Okay, when?"

A bell rang, and one of the other waitresses called out to her because an order was up.

"Tonight," he started as she walked away. When she looked back at him, Brady could see the guy on the other side of him listening to everything he was saying from his peripheral.

Cassie reached for two plates under the hot lamp and rested them in front of some men sitting at the counter down on the end, then walked his way again. Just the way she walked, even wearing a godawful mustard-color uniform, he swore her curves could've made a sack look tasteful. Her bust, her slim waist…

The other waitress on shift kept shooting a glance their way, Owen's way. Her expression seemed pissed, but Owen didn't seem to notice—or maybe he did, another brother who was damn hard to read.

"Tonight? I thought we were doing that thing tonight?" Cassie said, touching her face.

He could feel himself sweat, because "that thing" was just her and him in a bathtub, getting naked. With her bright, teasing blue eyes flickering with heat, she gave everything to him, and her smile was pure mischief. He wished he could walk out of the diner right now with his girl and forget lunch altogether.

"Well, we can do that later…but, you know, my family actually wants to meet my girlfriend," he finally said, as he knew Owen was waiting for him to get to it, already.

She leaned on the counter right in front of him, resting on her elbow, her chin on her palm, so close to him that she could have kissed him. He took in the teasing, and it seemed for a second that it was just her and him. He heard someone clear his throat and then nudge him again. Right, Owen.

Cassie pulled back. "Your girlfriend, huh? Sure, sounds fun."

"Great. I'll pick you up after I'm finished, about five? Then we'll head over."

Cassie gave him a big flirty smile from those lips he loved to kiss. Then she reached for the coffeepot and strode down the counter, refilling coffees down the line and talking to her other customers. That left him and his brother.

"Wow, for a second I thought I'd have to turn a hose on

you two," Owen said. "How long've you been seeing her? This is more than serious."

He had to fight the urge to look at his brother. When he did, he didn't miss the humor and teasing, but he was still feeling uncomfortable, just thinking of what it would be like that night to have everyone questioning Cassie and putting him on the spot.

Roasting and teasing were things he'd seen his brothers do well, and then there were Suzanne and Karen. He knew his sister and Jack would still be in town for another night or two. He'd be under the spotlight and questioned about Cassie in a way he'd never planned on.

"Oh, you know," he started, lifting his water and taking in her smile as she talked to some guy down at the end.

His shoulders tightened at the edge that seemed to come out of nowhere. He knew every guy there was imagining his hands on her, and he had to fight the urge to stand up and make it clear she was taken, because even though a number of guys here hit on her, it was him she'd gone out with.

"Six months, give or take, about as long as she's been in town," he said.

The other waitress, tall and skinny, who had been looking their way, was now behind the counter and reaching for the coffeepot. She walked toward them. "Well, didn't expect to see you in here, Owen," she said. "So how is Tessa? That's her name, right?"

She was looking down at Owen before looking over to Brady, and he realized there was history and maybe some bad blood there, too, but Owen was cool, calm, and all too together.

"Great, Lori," he said. "Tessa is fine. Thanks for asking." He said nothing else.

"So you work with Owen?" Lori said, turning to Brady in a way that had him feeling too much on the spot.

"Uh, yeah. I'm his brother, Brady." That was all he got out.

"Brady? Oh, yeah, you're the…"

He knew what she was about to say, because that was all the townspeople could talk about: Raymond O'Connell's other son, from the other woman, the one his father abandoned a wife and six kids for.

"Lori, great to see you again, but I think your customers are waiting," Owen cut in so Brady wouldn't have to answer.

She took the hint, made a face, and walked away, and he let out a breath, knowing the guy beside him was still listening.

"Well, that was awkward. Who was that?" he said in a low voice, turning to Owen.

Owen's expression was no longer amused or teasing but had suddenly turned so serious. "Someone I used to be involved with. She wanted more and didn't take it well when I said no, and we parted ways. Seems she still has a chip on her shoulder."

Owen pulled in a breath and reached for his glass of water, and he seemed to consider something before looking over to Brady again. "So, Cassie and Brady. Kind of has a nice ring to it. You've been seeing each other for six months, sneaking around? We knew you were smitten, but we had no idea you were so off the rails for that girl. Brady, Brady, Brady… Wow, can't wait until tonight, when we get to pry all the personal dirt from your girl. This should be interesting."

Brady just stared at Owen, knowing well that his brothers, his family, were about to make tonight a little too entertaining at his expense. For a moment, he worried that maybe, just maybe, it was a little too soon to bring Cassie to meet the O'Connells.

Her place was a three-story walk-up, an old building that had been converted into sixteen suites. Cassie's was a small one-bedroom filled with second-hand furniture. It was neat and tidy but dated, and that came with noisy plumbing, heating that didn't always work, and the ability to use only one electrical outlet at a time or a breaker would blow.

He slid his key into her lock and opened the door. "Cassie, you ready?" He closed it behind him, hearing the creak of footsteps from the apartment above.

"Just getting dressed," she called out, poking her head from the bedroom at the end. Her hair was pulled up in a messy bun, and she was wearing a cream lacy bra and blue jeans as she held up two shirts on hangers. "So which one do you think is more fitting to meet your family, the simple black V-neck, which is more conservative, or the purple flowers with ruffles, a little more dressy and sexy?"

Her eyes were teasing, but from the way she held up both, he realized she was serious. "It doesn't matter which one. It's just my family. Whichever one you want to wear will be fine."

She dropped her hands, the shirts and hangers slapping her thighs, and gestured with both again. "Seriously, Brady, it does matter. I'm a girl. I want to look nice, and you're not being helpful. Pick one, conservative or flirty." She gestured with both quite forcefully. Her expression had turned serious, and he realized she might be a little nervous, which was something he'd just never seen in her before.

"Well, the purple one will have my brothers all envying what a hottie I have, whereas the black one, as you say, is conservative—but I swear there's nothing you can't turn into a hot, classy number."

She tossed both onto the back of the sofa in the living room, which was two steps from her. "Ah, you know how to say all the right things."

She strode over to him, barefoot, sexy, and slid her arms over his shoulders. She went up on her toes as he slid his hands over her ass and pulled her against him. She pressed those warm lips to his and kissed him, and as she deepened the kiss, taking it from simple to scorching, he instinctively took a step with her, walking her backwards again to her bedroom, where he'd spent so many nights.

Her legs touched the edge of the double bed, which was neatly made with a faded floral comforter, and he had her lying back, running his hands over her curves, feeling the dip in her slim waistline, her flat stomach, as he pressed himself into her. He went to reach around and unhook her bra, pressing a kiss to her breasts through all that sexy lace. She was absolute perfection.

Her hands pressed into his chest and pushed him back, just enough that he could feel her putting the brakes on before he could have her stripped naked and under him in the next thirty seconds.

"Cool it, there," she said. "You said your family wants to meet me. I just had a shower, and I don't want to show up there looking as if I've just been fucked by you. It would make an already awkward night that much more so."

She somehow wiggled her way out from under him, and he wanted to weep, feeling his desire still very much there. It was almost agony.

"They'd never know," he said. "And who cares if they did, anyway? You think my brothers aren't getting the same thing? And…"

"And nothing, because that ain't happening, no way." She gestured to him, seeing that he couldn't hide his discomfort.

"So you expect me to go all night thinking about having you in bed? Denying me sex and making me wait… that's just cruel, Cassie."

She reached for the purple shirt and pulled it on, then walked over to the mirror and pulled the clip from her hair, letting her dark curls fall way past her shoulders. She turned to him as he took in the curve of her breasts and the cleavage of the fitted purple number, which only teased him. Damn, this was going to be a long, painful night.

"You know, maybe I misspoke," he said. "Why don't you wear the black shirt?"

Cassie shook her head gently and stepped closer, then leaned down, about to kiss him again. "No, I think I'll wear the purple one, because if I have to be uncomfortable in the hot seat, under the scrutiny of your family, meeting all of them, it will give me great pleasure knowing that you're suffering in your own discomfort all night."

She pressed her lips to him so lightly, so gently, teasing, then pulled back, her gaze heated. That one look would have him doing anything for her. "Besides, today was the first time you called me your girlfriend. Didn't realize we were putting a label on this." She stepped back.

As he lay on the bed, he felt himself backed into a wall, wondering for the first time whether she was on the same page. "Well…uh, we didn't really talk about where we are and everything…" was all he got out.

Mischief pulled at her lips again as she crossed her arms and lifted a brow, waiting for him to pull his foot out of his mouth.

"Well, no labels, but we're together, right?" he said. "I'm always here, and I have a key to your place, and there's no one else, so that makes you my girlfriend, I guess, and I'm your boyfriend."

She said nothing as he sat up on the bed.

"I am your boyfriend, right?" he said. "Seriously, Cassie, there's no one else?"

For those few seconds, he was kind of freaking out about what she'd say. Then she swept her fingers through her hair.

"Oh, relax, I just like seeing you sweat a bit. Yeah, I have eyes only for you, Brady. That's why you have a key to my place." She turned back to the mirror above the small dresser.

He took in the hamper of dirty clothes, seeing his blue and white shirt in there. A few of his clothes were here, but everything else was divided between Karen and Jack's place and Iris's, the places he lived that weren't really his.

"So why don't we make it more permanent?" he said.

She was brushing shadow on her eyelids. There was just something about watching her and everything she did; he could spend all day doing it and never get bored. To him, it seemed she never worried. She was confident, strong. She'd just arrived in town one day, not scared of anything.

"Make what permanent?" She gave him a distracted look as she reached for mascara and started applying it.

He could feel the tightness in his chest, the knot in his stomach. He was standing at the edge of a cliff, feeling the fear, but he didn't want to duck and run. He wanted to push through it, because there was something here that he wanted, something he had never experienced before.

"Well, I love you, Cassie," he said.

She paused, pulled the mascara away, and stuck the brush back in the tube. Her gaze softened as she put it down and turned to him, then stepped closer, right over to where he sat at the edge of the bed. She slid her hands over his cheeks.

"Hey, I love you too, but you're still not getting any before I meet your family tonight," she said, then pressed another kiss to his lips.

He took in the eyeshadow and light makeup that she didn't really need. When she pulled back, Brady found himself standing up, looking down at her, the top of her head, which came only to his chin. He slid his hands over her slender shoulders, feeling the way she breathed, the way she was standing with him in the silence. It wasn't just her energy or the way she spoke. Everything about her was a new experience.

"Well, I came here thinking of you and me not keeping two different places when we spend practically every other moment together. I mean, I keep my clothes somewhere else, but I sleep with you more nights than I don't, and those nights I'm not with you, all I can think of is being with you." He touched his tongue to his lips.

She shrugged. "Well, that was why I gave you the key. So you want to move in here with me?"

He realized that was what he'd wanted since the moment he walked in tonight, but he shook his head as he closed the distance to her and slid his hand to the small of her back, pulling her closer, lifting her chin with his other hand. He shook his head and said, "I'd like something a little more permanent than that."

Her face was an open question, and there was the flicker of something in her eyes. Maybe she understood what he was thinking when he dropped to his knee, his hand holding hers.

"What are you doing?" she said rather sharply—panicked, he thought.

"I knew, Cassie, the moment I saw you, that was it for me. There's just something about you. You take my breath away. You're all I think about when I'm working, and when I'm with you everything makes sense. When I see other guys in the diner drooling over you and eyeing you up, I want to drag each of them out and shout that you're mine, but I guess what I'm saying is I want you to marry me, to be my wife."

Her eyes widened, and she yanked her hand away. She stepped back from him. "Are you crazy, Brady? You just turned nineteen, and I'm only twenty. We haven't known each other that long. I barely know anything about you, and you know nothing of me. I'm only meeting your family tonight. This is insane. Brady, you aren't thinking clearly…" She was freaked out, mouth open as if she was thinking of what else to say as she gestured between them.

He stood up and took a step toward her. "Cassie, you know when you know. You really think waiting is going to make a difference? I don't care how young or old we are. This is right. I want you, I love you, and there's no one else. Let's do this, because I can honestly say you're the love of my life. I knew it the minute I saw you, and I'm more convinced now that this is right. Say yes? Come on, Cassie, marry me." He was right in front of her, his hands on her.

She just stared up at him. "But you don't know anything about me… Yes, the sex is great, and yes, I love you too, but, Brady, there's so much more. We don't know who we really are."

From the way she was talking, he realized she was trying to convince herself this couldn't work.

"We have a lifetime to get to know each other," he said. "But standing here with you, all I need to know is how I feel about you. We can talk about my family and my past, how I grew up, all the places I've lived, and your family and where you grew up, where you're from, but it doesn't change who you are or who I am. Come on…" He wouldn't let her pull her gaze from him.

She lifted her hands to her face, let out a breath, and shut her eyes for just a second. "You're crazy, Brady."

"Crazy for you and only you."

She hesitated. "So where's my ring?"

He knew he was wearing her down. "I'll pick one out tomorrow, and then we'll make it official. So is that a yes? You'll marry me, be my wife and spend a lifetime with me, grow old with me…?"

She slid her hands over his cheeks and lifted her gaze to him, her lips so close. "Yes, Brady, I'll marry you, even though this is crazy and you're out of your mind. But apparently so am I, since I just agreed…"

He kissed her before she could say anything else and lifted her, sweeping her in a circle. She squealed and he laughed. "You've made me so happy," he said. "We'll be crazy together, better together." He set her down, pulled her closer, and kissed her again. When he pulled back, she seemed to pull into herself a bit. "It's going to be great, you know."

She rubbed his chest and nodded. "We should get going to meet your family."

Right, his family. He couldn't wait to tell them, so happy that she'd agreed, and then get her back home tonight and never leave her bed again.

Yeah, this was going to be absolutely perfect.

Four

"I remember you said this car isn't yours," Cassie said. "It's Iris's, isn't it? How does she fit in again?"

Right, the sordid details of his family that he'd never discussed, because Raymond O'Connell no longer existed, *could* no longer exist, and he didn't know when he could share the truth of everything with her.

"She's my dad's first wife. They had six kids, who you'll meet tonight. Iris left me her car, and I stay at her house sometimes with my brother Luke when I'm not at my sister Karen's cramped condo, though she's left me the keys for it, because she and Jack are now in Missoula. He's going to be the next governor."

He glanced over to Cassie, who was in the passenger seat, her arms crossed. She turned, facing him, and he could see that her happy teasing had turned into something he couldn't put his finger on.

"But you'll like them," he said. "They're a fun bunch. Don't look so worried. Just wait until they hear about us. They'll be all over this, wanting to plan the wedding, host it, and…"

"About that, let's say we wait on telling everyone."

Something in her expression gave him a sinking feeling in his stomach. He was picking up on something. "Are you getting cold feet and wanting to back out?"

"No, it's not that. I just…" She pressed her lips together and shook her head. "It's nothing. Let's just not overwhelm your family. How about one step at a time, meeting them first? I mean, for all you know, they may not like me."

He wasn't sure where this was coming from. This was the first time he'd heard this kind of insecurity from her. "Don't be ridiculous. This is my family. I love you, so they'll love you. They're kind of crazy, but once you get to know all of them…" He pulled up in front of Marcus's house, behind the sheriff's cruiser.

She rested her hand on the dash and stared as he turned off the car. "Ah, the police are here…" She sounded off.

"Oh, didn't I tell you? My brother Marcus is the sheriff."

She dragged her gaze over to him, and the look in her blue eyes wasn't happy or teasing, as he'd expected. She shook her head as she unfastened her seatbelt and tossed him an odd look. "No, you failed to mention that. Any other secrets I should know about?" She gave the handle of the door a yank and pushed it open, then stepped out.

Brady followed her and gave the door a shove closed, his dark jacket unzipped, feeling the cold. She had shoved her hands in her coat pockets and was waiting for him to walk around the front of the vehicle, still staring at the sheriff's car. The sun had already dipped low, and it would be dark in about an hour, he thought.

"You worried about something?" he said. "You're not on some wanted list, are you?"

When she dragged her gaze over to him, she didn't smile, and he could see how off she was. "I'm not worried about anything, Brady. I just don't like surprises."

Whatever she meant by that, he wasn't sure.

"Well, as you said, there's a lot we don't know about each other—but we have time. And just think of how handy it is, having a sheriff in the family."

For a second, he thought he saw alarm or panic in her face. Maybe it was just that she was about to meet his family. Hell, he was nervous, bringing her.

"Hmm, well, let's just table that," was all she said.

He reached for her hand and started up the sidewalk, feeling his excitement and her tension. "You sure we can't tell them about us getting hitched?" He squeezed her hand.

She tossed him another gaze filled with alarm and panic. Her eyes widened, and her face paled. "Brady, no, please, not tonight. Let's just get through this. Let me meet your family and them me, and we'll do it another day. Okay?"

"All right, I won't say anything, so you can stop worrying. Don't be so nervous. It'll be fine. You already met Owen, and he thinks you're great," he said, though he wasn't sure she believed him as they strode up the steps.

"I think you're just saying that to make me feel better," she whispered.

He pulled open the door and dragged her inside, where he was greeted by Cameron, who was in his playpen in the living room, standing there, bouncing with a soother in his mouth. Marcus was standing over his son.

"Marcus, this is Cassie," Brady said. "Cassie, this is Marcus and my nephew, Cameron, and his wife, Charlotte."

"Hey, Cassie," Charlotte said. "It's great to meet you.

Come on in here and meet everyone. Don't worry—we're a great bunch. I can still remember the first time I had to meet the family. It was nerve-racking but relatively painless." Her long dark hair was pulled back in a ponytail, and she wore loose jeans and a striped T-shirt.

Brady took Cassie's coat, with its faux fur collar, and didn't miss the way Marcus took in her sexy shirt. He dragged his gaze to him as he tossed his coat with Cassie's over the chair. He could hear Luke and Ryan in the kitchen, and Suzanne too, and then he thought he heard Cassie's laughter.

"Wow, she's cute," Marcus said, striding over to him, and he wasn't sure what to make of his amused expression.

"Be nice," he said.

Marcus just crossed his arms, and Brady wasn't sure whether he was about to laugh. "Well, at least now I see what Owen was talking about."

He wasn't sure what Marcus meant by that, and he wasn't sure he wanted to know.

"Relax," Marcus said, then rested his hand on his shoulder and squeezed. "We're just having some fun at your expense."

"Well, consider this: She's nervous, so how about easing up a bit?"

The door opened behind him, and there were Karen and Jack, Jenny and Alison, and Harold, too.

"Hey, you," Karen whispered. "So is she here?"

He took in her dark hair, no red left at all. She slipped off her coat to reveal a black sweater and pants, whereas Jack wore the same style of dressy shirt and dark pants as always. He took Karen's coat from her.

"In the kitchen," he said. "Charlotte snagged her as soon as we walked through the door. Be nice and go easy. I want her to want to come back."

Karen just tapped his chest with the back of her hand as she started past him. "We're always nice," she said. "Stop worrying."

Jenny followed, and Marcus and Jack were over at the playpen, talking as Jack lifted Cameron, but Alison lingered a second. She wore the same heavy makeup as usual, but her dark hair was hanging long and loose, and she still had her coat on. She didn't seem ready to move, and the awkwardness set in again.

"Cassie is great," he said. "You'd like her." He realized how lame that sounded.

Alison dragged her gaze up to him, and he wasn't sure what to make of whatever was there in her brown eyes. Alison didn't fit into any mold. He understood her in a way few did, but at the same time, he'd never figured out how to get them to a point where they could be just friends.

"Tell me about her," she said.

That wasn't what he'd expected, and he didn't know what to say at first. "She works at Molly's diner. She moved here six months ago. She's got a great sense of humor, and she's confident and makes me laugh."

"So she's not from here?"

Brady was watching Cassie, seeing her laugh at whatever Karen and Suzanne were saying to her. It seemed she was holding her own. "No, I met her after she moved."

"Just her, no family?"

He wasn't sure what to make of the question. He dragged his gaze back to Alison. "Just her," he said.

They'd never talked about family, not really. He'd just mentioned his siblings, making sure the discussion never went to his dad and Iris. It was better that way.

"And where is she from?"

He looked back over to Cassie, trying to remember if he'd ever asked. She definitely wasn't one for talking about the personal side of things, either, but he thought she'd mentioned at some point that she was from back east. He knew he was frowning.

"We haven't really talked logistics about her family and mine, you know. It's safer that way," he added.

Alison nodded. "So, basically, you don't know anything about her," she said, then waited only another second before slipping off her coat, revealing a black velvet tank with a scoop neck. She walked away into the kitchen, and all Brady could do was stare.

He had asked Cassie to marry him, and she was meeting his family, but Alison's words hit home. He really didn't know anything about her, where she was from, who her parents were, where she grew up. Did she have any siblings?

All he'd done for the past six months was keep his own secrets while spending time with a girl he was head over heels for. The last thing he wanted was to talk about family, a subject he didn't talk about with strangers.

But she wasn't a stranger. He was going to marry her.

He didn't really know anything about her, but until now, it hadn't mattered.

CHAPTER

Five

H e was staring at a simple rock, a diamond in a gold band, with a tiny sticker price of over $4,999. For a moment, he was positive he'd stopped breathing as he stared in horror. Even though he didn't pay any rent, working for Owen wasn't making him rich.

He pulled in a sharp breath and held the ring back out to the lady behind the jewellery case. She had long, painted pink nails against her dark skin, and the wedding set on her finger was big and flashy.

"That's a little too much for me," he said. "Do you have something that doesn't cost that much?"

"You did say to show you an engagement ring a girl would want. This is what a girl wants." She gestured with the ring as if making her point. "If you think about it, it really is an investment. If you're concerned about the cost, we have all kinds of payment plans and financing options available, and jewellery, unlike other big-ticket items, actually appreciates in value."

He shook his head and kept shaking it until her smile

faded. He gestured to the glass case, which was filled with rings. "There's no way I can spend that much on a ring. A house is an investment, or a car, but not a ring. Something nice, please, but a little more reasonable."

She walked down to the end and shoved a key in the lock, then pulled out another ring. "So you're not really looking for a ring a girl would want," she said, and he sensed she was pissed off.

He took in the simple gold ring she walked back over to him. It was small, with the smallest diamond he'd ever seen. "And how much for this?"

She wasn't smiling anymore. "Two hundred and forty dollars. It's the cheapest we have if you want to stick with gold. You could also do gold plated, but I don't recommend that."

He really looked at the plain ring. It was gold, and there was a tiny diamond, so he held it closer, feeling the daintiness. He had no idea if it would fit as he did his best to picture it on Cassie's finger.

He dragged his gaze back down to the case where the big rock with the huge price tag sat amongst a bunch of other impressive rings that looked similarly way too expensive. Okay, so that was the section of the shop that was out of the question.

"I'll take this one," he said. "Although that ring is nice, we're just starting out, and I'm not going broke over a ring. I know Cassie will love this one."

He hoped she would, but as he considered the ring and paid for it, he realized this was just one more thing about Cassie that he didn't really know. She had never seemed to be into the glitz and flash, though.

He tucked the ring box into his down jacket pocket and took in the darkened diner just up the block as he walked out of the store. The diner would be closed for the night, and he pictured Cassie waiting for him at her place—no, their place.

He pulled open the door to Iris's Subaru, seeing the tool belt on the passenger seat, a gift from his brothers. Just then, his phoned dinged, a text from Ryan, asking if he would be coming over that night.

He just shook his head as he climbed behind the wheel, sending back a quick text: *Not tonight.* He had plans, and they didn't include another night of his family questioning his girl and poking fun at him, with him worrying about what they'd say to embarrass him. His family had had their fun.

Still, Alison's words continued to run through his mind. What did they really know about each other?

Not much.

Maybe tonight they'd talk, and he'd ask her about her family, where she grew up—and then he'd figure out what to say about Raymond. He really should talk to his dad or maybe Luke first, considering Luke had been the one to drill into him that Raymond O'Connell was now officially dead.

It didn't take him long to pull up in front of Cassie's building, and he found a spot on the street and tucked his toolbelt and brand-new tools under the back seat, out of sight. He reached for the small canvas bag of clothes and essentials he'd grabbed from Iris's earlier that day and then locked up the car before he strode up the steps to the front door.

When he pulled it open, he was instantly blasted by a wave of unusual heat, and he took in the narrow hallway and the stairs that led up to the second floor. The floorboards squeaked on the stairs, and he shoved his key in the lock of her door, stepping into the darkness. He flicked on the light. "Cassie, you here?"

He closed the door, feeling the same heat in the suite, and he shrugged out of his coat and hung it on the hook beside the green sweater she often wore. The thermostat was set at the same sixty-five it always was, and he listened, hearing nothing. Maybe she was sleeping, considering all they'd done when they got home the night before was find their way to bed, where the sex had been off the charts.

He thought it had been after two or three that he'd fallen asleep. She'd kissed him to wake him at dawn, already dressed and ready for her early shift at the diner.

"Cassie, I think the heat's broken or something," he called out as he started into the bedroom, which was dark. He flicked on the light, seeing the empty bed just as he'd left it, unmade, with their clothes from last night still in a heap on the floor. He reached for them, his shirt, her jeans and underwear, and tossed them in the hamper.

As he strode into the kitchen, starting to sweat from the heat, he flicked on the light and saw her coffee mug still in the sink, as was his juice glass from that morning. It didn't look as if she'd ever come home after work, or maybe she had left because of the heat. He pulled out his cell phone, leaning against the kitchen counter, and dialed her number, but it went right to her generic voicemail.

"Hey, I'm home, but you're not here," he said. "The heat is all wonky. Let me know if you already called the super. If not, I'll head down and have a word with him. The apartment feels like we're in the tropics. I'm going to be shedding clothes here really quick…so call me back."

He rested his phone on the counter and waited a second for her to call back, staring at the screen, but nothing. Maybe she was at the store, picking up dinner? He pulled open the fridge, seeing the usual stuff, peanut butter, condiments, pickles, and leftover sandwich meat, lettuce, and cheese. He closed it, knowing he'd have to open the windows soon to cool the place down.

He shoved his phone in his pocket and pulled the keys from his jacket, then stepped out of the apartment and strode down the stairs to the first floor, down the narrow hall to the suite at the end, which he knew belonged to the building manager.

He fisted his hand and knocked, hearing a TV inside and then footsteps before the door opened, and he took in a dark-haired man with a pot belly in a dingy white tank top. He appeared grungy, as if he hadn't bothered shaving, exercising, or doing much of anything. He was short, and Brady towered over him, though he thought the man might be close to his dad's age.

"What?" was all the man said, staring at Brady with a look he knew creeped Cassie out.

"Hey, the heat in here is over the top," Brady said. "I'm in the suite upstairs with Cassie Arnold. I'm her fiancé, Brady. We have the same ridiculous heat that's in the hallway, and our thermostat is set at only sixty-five."

The man just stared. He had dark eyes and didn't smile, giving the impression that this was a petty problem he wasn't about to address. "It's an old building, and it's on a boiler that doesn't always work. I'll have someone look at it tomorrow." He went to shut the door.

Brady slapped his hand to the door before he could slam it in his face. "Do you have any idea how hot it is in here? It has to be close to eighty or ninety degrees. How about getting someone in here tonight?"

All the man did was stare at him and then at his hand pressed to the door, so Brady pulled his hand away. The man made a face and shook his head. "Not happening. The owner isn't spending money on an overtime call, and his handyman isn't available to look at it tonight."

He stared at the man. "You know rent could be withheld if you're not going to fix it."

Not even a smile. He realized the man was going to close the door in his face. "You don't pay rent, you don't have a roof. Those locks can easily be changed, and I can and will do it, and you'll find your things dumped outside on the sidewalk. So do not threaten me. It will be fixed when it's fixed. Who are you, again?"

Okay, maybe not the smartest thing he'd done.

"Brady Baker. I'm Cassie Arnold's fiancé, suite 206." He gestured upstairs.

The man narrowed his eyes. "Oh, right, the cute girl. I didn't know there was a second occupant. That could be a problem."

Brady swore under his breath. The super was an asshole.

"We'll have to see what the owner says about that, but an extra occupant means an extra fee will apply. Now get your hand off my door. The heat will be fixed when it's fixed, so don't come down here again, issuing threats."

Then the man shut the door in his face, and Brady just took in the old building, thinking maybe it was time he looked for something better for him and his girl.

As he walked to the stairs and pulled out his phone, he saw there were no missed calls, no voicemails. Where was Cassie, exactly?

He started up the stairs, hearing noise from another suite. He was beginning to sweat again. Maybe they should stay at Iris's tonight, and then he'd give her the ring and celebrate, and then, tomorrow, they'd tell his family.

He stopped halfway up the stairs and looked back to the front door, the empty front door. All he could do was wonder where Cassie had gone.

CHAPTER

Six

B rady glanced from the ring in the black velvet jewelry box on the kitchen counter to the clock on the stove. It was now after eleven.

He stared at the sandwich he'd made for Cassie, still sitting on its plate. His cell phone was lying beside it, the screen black even though he expected it to ring anytime. He willed it to ring.

"Cassie, where are you?" He fisted his hand and hit the counter, but it did nothing to take the edge off his worry.

He finally reached for the plate, opened the fridge, and slid the sandwich inside on the top shelf beside the peanut butter and half a block of cheddar, then reached over his shoulder and neck and pulled at the tension there.

He just stood there another second before grabbing his phone and pulling up his brothers' numbers, Ryan, Luke, Owen, and then Marcus. His thumb hovered, and then he dialed. It had barely rung once when he heard Luke's deep voice.

"What's going on?"

Brady could hear the TV in the background. "I hope I'm not worrying for nothing, but I can't find Cassie," he said. "She hasn't come home yet. This isn't like her." He wondered how to explain that this wasn't right, seeing as his brothers had just met her.

"Maybe she had second thoughts about you moving in with her and she's out with friends now, enjoying her freedom," Luke said.

Brady pulled the phone away and stared at it. "Uh, no. Seriously? Cassie wouldn't do that." He shook his head and rubbed his hand over it. "You don't know her. I don't even think she has friends, considering I've never seen her go out with someone else. She's always here at home. But to tell you the truth, I don't think she ever came home from the diner today."

He was walking into the bedroom and flicked on the light again, seeing the unmade bed but not her godawful mustard uniform, which she would've tossed there. "I've called her over and over, and she hasn't called me back. This isn't like her."

Luke sighed. "Hang tight. I'll be right over." Then he was gone with a click.

Brady took in the closet, seeing the other dress uniform on a hanger. The small closet was mostly empty. Cassie just didn't have a lot of clothes.

He squeezed his phone, taking in the screen. She still hadn't called, so he walked out of the bedroom and flicked off the light, then rested the phone back on the counter in the kitchen.

He glanced at the bag of clothes and essentials that he'd tossed on the floor by the door when he walked in, then walked over to the open window. Iris's Subaru was parked under the streetlight, and he spotted a few other cars and could hear the sounds of the night from the open window. The cold breeze was welcome over the heat that continued to blast.

He wasn't sure how long he stood there before he heard footsteps on the stairs outside, then a knock at the door. For a second, his heart filled with hope, and he strode over to it and pulled it open only to see Marcus. His hair had that bedhead look, and he wore his sheriff's jacket. Luke was there too in a heavy coat, his dark hair pulled back in a ponytail.

His heart sank.

"Take it she's still not here," Luke said and stepped in first.

Marcus gave him one of his looks and rested a hand on his shoulder, looking around at everything, considering he'd never been there before.

"It's hotter than Hades in here," Luke said, tapping the thermostat. "You got the heat cranked?"

"Seems to be an issue with the boiler or something," Brady said. "I already had a word with the super downstairs, who isn't too inclined to fix it or anything. Seems to be one thing after another with this place. It's old, rundown. Was going to suggest to Cassie that we stay at Iris's tonight. You wouldn't mind, would you?"

Luke was still standing at the thermostat. "It's your home too," he said. "You don't have to ask."

"So this is where you've been spending all your nights," Marcus said as Brady walked toward him into the kitchen, which was really part of the living room. "You're living with Cassie now?"

It seemed Luke had brought Marcus up to speed. Back at Iris's, while packing his bag, he had explained that he was moving in with Cassie, but that had been pretty much it for the conversation.

"Was always here anyways and stayed over most nights," Brady said. "Just seemed easier to have everything here. I see Luke called you and pulled you from bed?" Okay, that sounded lame.

"Yeah, he said you were worried about Cassie, that she didn't come home. Pretty sure I said in our sit-down that you can call if there's a problem. Our house is early to bed, with kids who are up at the crack of dawn." Marcus looked at him. "So Cassie hasn't come home, and you're sounding the alarm. Did you call any of her friends?"

What was he supposed to say? He'd already told Luke she just didn't have any friends to go out with. She never had the entire time they'd been together. So he shook his head. "Cassie has been in town only six months, and we've kind of been together the entire time. She's never gone out with a friend. Look, she's not answering her phone, and that's not like her. She'd have told me."

Luke was in the kitchen at the counter, looking at everything, opening cupboard doors. What he was looking for, Brady had no idea. He pulled open the fridge.

"Luke, she's not in the kitchen," he said with a ton of sarcasm before turning back to Marcus.

"Brady, I know you like Cassie," Marcus said. "I could see it last night when you brought her over. But you haven't really known her that long, and we've just met her. She seems like a nice girl, but what do you really know about her? Does she really not have any friends?"

He wanted to say no, he was sure, but he found himself shrugging instead. "I don't know," he said. "I don't think so. Look, I just want to find her. She has the people she works with at the diner, but she's never gone out with them. I'm pretty sure she didn't come home from the diner today. She has two uniforms, and only one is here, and everything is how it was left this morning. She was gone before me, so…"

He stopped talking. He didn't know how to explain any of it to cop Marcus, who was staring at him, asking the kinds of questions he didn't know how to answer. "Look, the thing is that I've called her and called her, and she's not answering, and she hasn't called back. So yeah, I'm worried. Overreacting? I hope so, but I don't think so."

"So she could be out with someone and you just don't know it?" Marcus said. "Someone from the diner, maybe. Did you call the diner? Hanging around late after closing, talking… Those are possibilities. Maybe she went out for dinner with someone from work, at their place, and she lost track of time, or her cell phone died and she hasn't noticed."

What was he supposed to say? They could list all the possible scenarios he hadn't considered, but they didn't seem plausible. "The diner closes early, and she's never stayed after before. She goes to work and then comes home. She's never gone out with someone from the diner. I don't even think she's friends with any of them."

Luke was now in the bedroom, and the light was on. It seemed he was looking at everything. He flicked the light off and walked back out.

Marcus pressed his cell phone to his ear. "Well, I'll call. She's probably still there," he said. He put it on speaker, and Brady could hear the ringing and ringing, but no one answered. Apparently, the diner didn't even have voicemail.

"You know, Brady, I hate to say this, but you're probably overreacting," Marcus said. "She's likely over at a friend's from work, and from what you're saying, it doesn't sound like you know much about her. It's not as if she's missing. If someone sounded the alarm every time I stayed out too late at your age, they'd have been looking for me every night. That old adage about crying wolf comes into play. How about you don't panic and give her some space? Let me tell you something about women: Sometimes they want another woman to talk to. I'm sure she'll show up, and if she doesn't come home tonight, the simple explanation is that she stayed over at a friend's—or maybe she's seeing someone else."

He couldn't believe Marcus had said that.

Luke was in the kitchen again now, holding the ring box in his hand, and he flicked it open. He stared at it, then lifted his gaze and slid it over to him. Those O'Connell blue eyes reminded him so much of his dad's, with that same questioning gaze that demanded an answer. "And this is?"

"An engagement ring," he said, dragging his gaze from Luke to Marcus, who wasn't trying to hide his surprise. "Look, you should know that I asked Cassie to marry me yesterday, and she said yes. I picked up the ring after work. I was planning on giving it to her tonight, but here we are."

He wasn't sure what to make of the exchange between Luke and Marcus. Luke turned the ring box over, then held it up and showed it to Marcus before closing it and putting it down.

"You asked her to marry you," was all Marcus said. "Well, then I think you need to consider something, because from where I'm standing, it seems maybe someone got cold feet, is panicking, and is likely having second thoughts. You're both kids…"

Brady just stared at Marcus and then dragged his gaze back over to Luke, feeling that fiery anger beginning to build in his stomach. His brothers didn't get it. "It seems you've already made your mind up about Cassie, about me

—but make no mistake. I love her, and she loves me, and she wouldn't just take off. I know her."

Marcus took a step toward him and rested a hand on his shoulder, shaking his head. "Well, that's the thing, Brady. I don't think you do, not really."

So that was it. "Well, thanks for not helping," he said.

Luke sighed. "We never said we're not about to help, Brady, so dial back all that outrage and attitude. Chances are she's going to come walking through that door anytime, and then you're going to feel like a complete jackass for sounding the alarm, because that kind of over-reaction with a girl can have her booting you out and ending whatever this thing is between you two right quick. Just FYI, you're both young, and you getting your shorts in a knot over the simple questions we're asking tells me one thing: You don't know anything about this girl.

"Trying to play house at your age is exactly what you shouldn't be doing," Luke continued. "I have to ask you this, Brady. Getting married at your age, are you sure this is the wisest choice? If she doesn't walk through that door, you need to figure out what you do know about her. Everyone has someone, family, a person to call, and everyone has secrets, yet you're standing here, freaking out, mad at us because we're asking you the kinds of things you should know.

"Having said that, I bet anything she's going to walk through that door soon, or she came home to this hotbox and decided to go stay at a friend's, someone you evidently don't know. Regardless, I think you two need to sit down and have a talk about the things you don't know about each other."

Luke was so matter of fact as he set the ring down on the counter, and Brady couldn't help feeling as if he'd just been scolded like a little kid. But then, Luke never had sugar-coated anything.

"That was the plan for tonight, to talk to her about her family, where she's from," Brady said. "But at the same time, you know why we haven't talked about it yet. It's because I can't talk about Raymond, you know, good old Dad, who doesn't exist, or how I grew up, or who he is. So why would I question her about her family when I'm not talking about mine? I steered clear of that territory. She knows about you, my siblings, but that's it. She moved here six months ago. We talk about the present, not our pasts. So if either of you have any ideas of what I should've said, I'd love to hear it, because I've been wrestling with it all day."

Marcus winced as if maybe, just maybe, he now understood.

"You know you can't say anything," Luke said from behind him.

Brady didn't nod as he pulled in a breath, stepping back so he could see Luke, as well. "I figured as much, but at the same time, is it always going to need to be a secret? When we get married, when she becomes a part of this family, is there not a point where she can know? Charlotte, Jenny, Tessa, Harold, and Jack all know."

Luke and Marcus just stared at each other.

"I understand what you're saying, but that's different," Marcus said.

Brady crossed his arms and looked over to Luke, whose gaze lingered on Marcus before shifting to him.

"Marcus is right to a point," Luke said. "You just met Cassie. Right now, she can't know because she isn't a part of the family. Charlotte, Jenny, Tessa, Harold, and Jack are. One day, it may be different, and we'll talk then about what you can and can't say. But right now I think there are more pressing questions, like where Cassie is and why you need to get married to a girl who, by your own admission, you don't seem to know anything about."

What could he say? His brothers, he realized, still saw him as a kid.

Brady blinked awake, hearing his phone ringing from where he'd apparently fallen asleep on the sofa. He tossed the blanket aside in the now freezing apartment. The sun was coming up, and he could see his breath fog in the air.

"Cassie!" he called out, but he heard nothing other than silence in the apartment as he reached for his cell phone on the back of the sofa. "Hello?" He pressed his hand to his face.

"Hey, heard about last night from Marcus," Owen said.

Brady didn't even know what time it was. He walked over to the window to close it. "I must have fallen asleep. What time is it?" he said, feeling the tiredness in his voice as he walked into the bedroom, expecting to see Cassie in bed but finding it unmade and empty, exactly how it had looked since yesterday.

"Seven thirty," Owen said.

Brady's heart sank. He strode into the hall and took in the open darkened bathroom. Not even her coat was hanging at the front door. "She's still not here," Brady said.

"She didn't come home, by the looks of it." He gestured to the door.

"Listen, do you know who she may have stayed with?" Owen said.

Brady took in the ring box on the counter. The clock on the stove said 7:35 a.m. It had been after three when Luke left, though Marcus had left at midnight. When had he fallen asleep? Maybe around four.

"I have no idea," he said, dragging his hand over his face. "I'll try calling her again, see if she answers. Or maybe I'll swing by the diner this morning…"

"That's why I'm calling," Owen said. "Lori called me from the diner. Apparently, Cassie didn't show up for her breakfast shift at six. Lori said she tried calling her cell phone and got no answer. She remembered meeting you with me yesterday and put everything together, knowing you're seeing Cassie, though apparently that's all anyone at the diner knows about her."

That had Brady just staring at the closed window. He couldn't feel any heat at all now in the apartment, so he walked over to the thermostat and turned it up, though he was sure it would do nothing. The damn thing was broken.

"I don't know what to say," he finally replied. "Marcus grilled me about her last night and suggested some things. You sure she's not at work?"

"Yeah, Lori wouldn't call me otherwise," Owen said. "I told her I'd call you and find out what's what, but Marcus called me a minute ago before I could and told me about you all looking for Cassie last night. I was hoping she'd have shown up."

There was a knock at the door, and all he could think was that it was Cassie, and maybe she'd lost her key or something.

"Someone's at the door," Brady said. When he pulled it

open, he saw that it was Marcus in his sheriff's jacket and duty belt, ready for work. "It's Marcus."

"Okay, listen, I'm on my way over," Owen said, then hung up.

Brady stepped back, holding up his phone, feeling the disappointment.

"I take it she's not here," Marcus said as he stepped inside.

Brady just shook his head, running his hand over his hair. "No. I fell asleep and just woke up, and she's not here. Was hoping that was her at the door. She didn't come home. Owen said he got a call from someone at the diner."

"Yeah, Lori, an old jilted flame," Marcus said, striding into the kitchen and living room, taking in the blanket on the old sofa, which hadn't really been that comfortable. "Freezing in here now. So she didn't show up for work, either, and you have no idea where she could've gone?"

He just shook his head. He was shivering now, so he strode back to the door and reached for his down coat to pull it on. Marcus was over by the window now, looking around at the sparse furnishings.

"I'm at a loss," Brady said. "Something has to have happened, Marcus. She didn't show for work, and she didn't come home from work, either. Maybe something happened there. I think I'm going to go down to the diner and talk to them, find out who last saw her. Maybe she said something to one of them."

Marcus had his arms crossed and said nothing for a second, giving him everything, though Brady wasn't in the mood for that O'Connell look this morning.

"What?" he snapped.

"Hey, just cool it," Marcus said. "Dial it back. I understand your frustration, but there has to be an explanation, so let me go down to the diner and have a word with Lori and Frank, who owns the place. Maybe you're right that she said something to one of them. Before you start freaking out, let's trace her steps."

Maybe Marcus was finally hearing him.

"Great, good," Brady said. "Just let me…" He was going to say "change," but why bother? He turned to the bedroom and felt a hand on his shoulder.

"Look, you stay here," Marcus said. "I'll go down and have a talk with them. It would be better if you weren't there."

Brady was already shaking his head. "No, I'm coming too. She's my fiancée. Seriously, I'm not some kid. I'm nineteen. I'm tired of being treated as if I can't handle anything."

Marcus lifted his hands in the air as if surrendering, and he seemed to consider his words for a second. "I'm not doing that, Brady. Please understand, if something has happened to Cassie, this is police business now, and you can't be involved. You'll have to sit back just like everyone else while I investigate. What if she shows up and you're not here? Have you thought of that?"

He shut his eyes against the tiredness and worry that were fogging his brain. "Okay, but the thing is, Marcus, she didn't show up for work, and she didn't come home last night. I'm not sitting here waiting, because I'll go out of my mind. I'm coming." He stepped back and shoved his hands in his pockets, feeling his keys, the ones Cassie had given him.

"Fine, then let's go," Marcus said and started to the door.

Brady shoved on his sneakers where he had kicked them off the night before, and Marcus pulled open the door and stepped out. He looked back to him and nodded.

Brady followed and pulled the door closed and locked

it behind him. They were halfway down the stairs when he spotted Owen at the door of the building. Right, he'd forgotten he was on his way over.

"You find her?" was all Owen said.

"No, we're headed to the diner," Marcus said. "Brady insisted on coming."

Owen's gaze lingered a second, and then he nodded. "Good idea. Maybe someone there knows something." He followed them out of the building and then settled his hand on Brady's shoulder.

"Don't worry about the job site today," Owen said. "I'll handle things. You just find her and let me know if you hear something."

He turned to head back toward his plumbing van, whereas Marcus was already at the sheriff's car, his door open, standing there, resting his arms on the roof of the vehicle.

Brady walked over to the passenger side and pulled open the door, then stared at his brother, the cop. He was feeling a lot of things, mostly fear, which he had never felt so strongly before. "Marcus, what if something's happened to her?"

Marcus pulled in a breath and exhaled in the frosty morning air. "Let's not automatically jump to the worst-case scenario. There could be a simple explanation, okay?"

Brady didn't know why, but he had this feeling that whatever had happened wasn't anything simple. He just hoped, though, that he was wrong.

T he diner was hopping with the early breakfast crowd as he followed Marcus, who turned to him, gestured, and said, "Coffee?"

He just shook his head, wondering why Marcus hadn't noticed yet that Brady never drank coffee. He was more into juice, orange or grapefruit. Even Cassie had figured out that quirk.

He looked around at the breakfast the diner was serving everyone. Normally, he'd be starving, but maybe it was his worry for Cassie that made him think he couldn't eat a thing. The only thing he wanted was to find her.

He searched the diner, expecting to see her come out of the back room as he stared at the swinging door. Marcus was still standing there, right in front of him, waiting for Lori, who was carrying two plates. She gestured to Marcus with her chin. Owen's ex-girlfriend was apparently the one who had called that morning, looking for Cassie.

She strode their way, her pace fast.

"Thanks so much for calling Owen this morning, Lori,

and letting us know about Cassie," Marcus said, pulling out a notepad. "So she didn't show for her shift?"

Lori seemed surprised that Marcus was there, he thought. Brady had seen Lori so many times before, but until yesterday, he'd had no idea of her past with Owen. Her hair was brown, tied back in a ponytail, and she had freckles. She was tall and thin. She wasn't the kind of woman who stood out, and he was having a hard time picturing her with Owen, especially after having met Tessa: blond, pretty, quirky, and so much his other half.

She was nodding. "She works the morning shift, and she hasn't been here that long, but this is the first time she's just not showed. This was my day off, and I didn't appreciate the early-morning call in."

He didn't miss her annoyance at being put out.

"I don't know what's up," she continued, "but I'd have appreciated a heads-up if she was going to pull this. I'm not really impressed. You know, the fact that she couldn't pick up the phone and let us know…"

He wondered if she had gone on and on like this with Owen, because she was beginning to really piss him off. He fisted his hands in his pockets. The tension was thick across his neck and shoulders, pulling again as he fought the urge to set her straight.

Maybe Marcus knew, as he tossed him a glance over his shoulder. "So what you're saying, Lori, is that no one knows anything. She didn't mention to anyone that she wouldn't be coming in? She doesn't have any friends here? Did something happen yesterday, or are you sure she didn't go out with someone from the diner last night?"

Brady's hands were still shoved in the pockets of his jacket. He wasn't sure what to think as he looked around.

Lori was shaking her head. "No, Cassie has kind of always kept to herself. You know, a few of us go out after the diner closes, and she's been invited, but she's always said no. No one here has heard from her. She said nothing. But I don't understand why you're here, Marcus. Did something happen?"

"That's the thing, Lori. We don't know," Marcus said. "She hasn't been seen since yesterday. She was at work, right?"

Lori dragged her gaze from Marcus over to Brady and back. He could see the moment she realized maybe there was a problem. Then some man, the manager or a cook from the back, called her name, and she turned and gestured. "Look, I have orders up, and I have to get back to it, but she was here yesterday, yes. Unusually quiet, though. Come to think of it, she kept getting calls on her cell phone. Frank even said something to her at one point. Whoever it was who called her, I don't think she was happy about it. I can't remember seeing her so off."

Brady didn't know why, but just hearing that bothered him in ways he couldn't have explained. "And she didn't say who it was?" he jumped in.

Marcus only glanced his way for a second. Standing next to his brother, he realized everyone in the place was watching. Apparently, having a sheriff walk in and talk to someone was big news. He heard a ding again.

"Look, I've really got to get back to work, but as I said, she always did her job. The customers loved her. For a waitress, she was pretty good, and she showed every day until this morning. But she didn't talk about herself. I don't know what's going on, but if she doesn't show again, she's out of a job. Frank is not going to keep her." Then Lori hurried away, back to the hot plate, where orders were waiting for her.

Marcus took a second to really look at him and said, "Any idea who she would've been talking to?"

They strode out of the diner, back to the sheriff's cruiser, and just stood there for a second, taking in downtown, the cold stinging his ears. He could use a hot shower, but only after he found out what had happened to Cassie.

"I don't know," Brady said. "I was working with Owen all day and then stopped to buy the ring. I called her I don't know how many times last night, and she never called back. I didn't stop for lunch yesterday because the job was way out of town, and we worked right through. I have no idea who she would've been talking to. It makes absolutely no sense to me. I have more questions now than answers."

"Excuse me," someone interrupted them. "You were asking about Cassie?"

Brady turned to see a man emerging from the diner. He wore a long dirty apron, and he wasn't sure, but he thought he'd seen him a time or two in back. A dishwasher, a line cook? Maybe.

"And you are?" Marcus stepped over to the man, glancing only once to Brady.

"Tyler Chapman," he said. "I work in back in the kitchen. Lori said you were asking about Cassie. Is she missing?"

Brady found himself really looking at this guy, unshaven, tall, and lanky, with a chipped tooth, from what he could see. "I'm her fiancé," Brady said. "She didn't come home last night, but she was at work yesterday. Did she say where she was going when she left?"

He was done being a sidekick, because he wanted some answers, and he wasn't sure he was getting any. Definitely not the ones he wanted.

"She closed up and left before me," Tyler said. "She did seem unusually distracted, though. Didn't know she was getting married. Seen you in the diner all the time, and she didn't say you were an item."

What was it about Tyler that he didn't like? He wasn't old, maybe closer to Marcus's age, but he knew when a guy was interested in a girl, and this guy seemed too interested.

"We are an item. We're getting married." He wasn't sure why he needed to make that point very, very clear.

"Did Cassie say anything about where she was going when she left work?" Marcus asked.

Tyler stepped closer, and Brady could see the people inside the diner watching shamelessly through the window, likely coming up with their own stories about why they were there. He realized Tyler still hadn't answered, and he worried that he knew more about Cassie than he did, the kinds of things he should know.

"She didn't really say anything," Tyler said. He had a tattoo of a dagger on his forearm, he noticed. "I know I asked her yesterday if everything was okay because of how off she seemed. She said not to worry about it. But that's Cassie for you."

"So she didn't tell you where she was going and that she wouldn't be coming into work today?" Marcus said.

Tyler just shrugged. "No, she said nothing about taking today off. She did, though, say that a problem came up that she had to handle. That was after Frank got mad at her. I asked her if she was okay, and she just offered me that smile she has, but I could see something was off. Cassie didn't talk about herself like other women here. She did her job. She was dependable. Maybe she went back home. Maybe it was a family problem that came up, or something happened."

Marcus adjusted his stance. Brady knew nothing about her family.

"Did Cassie talk to you about a family problem?" Marcus said. "Did she have family?"

Tyler dragged his gaze from Marcus to Brady and then back. "I just know she mentioned one time where she was from. I don't even remember how it came up, but it was some tiny place in Minnesota…Ely. She didn't talk about them, but I just assumed she had family. I'm trying to think, but it was some time ago. Cassie was pretty noncommittal. That's all I can say. I hope everything's all right. Is she missing?"

Brady knew he was looking for more.

"She told you she was from Ely, Minnesota?" Marcus asked. "She said nothing else about family, parents, sisters, brothers, maybe an old boyfriend? Did she mention any problems or reasons why she moved here?"

Tyler shot him a big-eyed look as if he realized there could be a problem. "No, as I said, Cassie was pretty quiet. Lori was going on about Cassie getting calls yesterday, and I remember Frank did yell at her once to get off the phone, and that was when I asked her if everything was okay. She was upset, too, which isn't like Cassie. I'm pretty sure whoever it was, she didn't want them calling."

So who was calling her? Brady didn't have a clue.

"You didn't answer me before," Tyler said. "Has something happened to Cassie?"

Marcus gave a tight smile and jutted his chin back to the restaurant. "Not sure. She didn't come home last night. It could be nothing, but if you think of something, give me a call." He pulled out a card from his pocket and handed it to Tyler, who gestured with it and then stepped back to the diner.

"You think he knows more?" Brady said.

Marcus gave him a look that reminded him of his dad when he was considering what to say or not say. "What I think is that Cassie had some secrets, big secrets. I'd like to know who was calling her. You didn't know about a place in Ely, Minnesota?"

His chest ached, hearing things about Cassie for the first time. He felt as if a big part of her life was a secret. "No, I didn't. So what now?"

Marcus only nodded, reached over, and touched his shoulder before walking around to the driver's side of the cruiser. "We'll start with finding out who called her. You're going to give me her cell phone number, and I'll find out. Then we'll find her."

Brady just stood there for a second as his brother opened his door. "You think it'll be that easy?"

Marcus shook his head. "No, but if I've learned anything being a cop, it's that nothing should surprise me."

Brady wasn't sure what to make of that. The only thing he wanted was to find Cassie, and it bothered him more than anything to know that someone had been calling her and upset her. Whatever was going on, he hoped it was something small.

But something about all of this made him unable to shake the feeling that finding her wasn't going to be easy.

Nine

"Ely, Montana," Marcus said. "That's right."

Sitting in an uncomfortable wood chair across the desk, Brady just stared at his brother on the phone. Who he was talking to, he had no idea. The door was open, and Harold walked in, carrying a coffee.

"Here, you sure you don't want a coffee? You should have something to eat, too. I can send out for something." Harold was holding the coffee out to him, but he set it on the desk when he didn't take it.

Brady just stared at the steaming mug and then dragged his gaze back to Harold. "No, I'm good…" he started.

"Order him a ham and cheese," Marcus said, sliding the phone from his mouth. "Get Colby to run down and pick it up."

Harold patted his shoulder. "Marcus is right. You need to eat. Look, don't worry. We'll track her down. And get some caffeine into you. You look like you need it."

Brady took in Suzanne's partner, another cop in the

family, then just stared at the coffee again, wondering why everyone assumed he drank it.

There was a knock on the open door, and he saw the dispatcher who had replaced Charlotte. Therese was standing there in her deputy uniform. He'd seen her only a few times. Her dark hair was cut short, and she was slim, and she had a nice smile, but he knew nothing about her. There was a scar below her eye, he noticed. It was faint on her dark skin.

"Sheriff, got a name for you on the number that called the cell phone," she said, holding a paper.

Harold walked over and took it, then said something to her, and she nodded. It seemed they worked well together. He hadn't heard too much about the situation with the politics at the sheriff's office. He knew Charlotte still wasn't working, and the election for a new sheriff had been postponed until the spring. It wasn't really something they had talked too much about as of late.

Brady wasn't sure how to feel. Right now, he just wanted someone to find Cassie.

Marcus hung up the phone and strode over to Therese and Harold. "Good work, Therese. Listen, can you tell Colby to run out and grab a sandwich for Brady—and some juice, as well? Orange, right?"

It took Brady a second before he nodded and shrugged, realizing maybe Marcus had been paying attention.

Therese nodded and left, and Harold handed the paper over to Marcus.

Brady wanted to yell because no one was saying anything, and for a moment, he thought both Marcus and Harold would share nothing. Something seemed to pass between them, that silent cop thing they did way too often, as if they didn't need to speak because they knew what the other was thinking, just like a married couple.

"Seriously, you two, if you found out who called Cassie, then tell me already," Brady said. "This isn't a secret. Don't keep it from me."

Marcus lifted his gaze, and Harold was watching him, arms crossed. Standing next to his brother, he seemed formidable

"You know anyone by the name of Jade Arnold?" Marcus finally said. "Cassie's last name is Arnold, right?"

Brady sat up. "Yeah, that's her last name. Who is Jade? Did you find that out, or do you have something else? That's who called Cassie yesterday?"

"From Cassie's phone records, it seems she called six times yesterday but never before that. Another thing, too: You said Cassie moved here six months ago and you met her at the diner then?"

He found himself waiting, feeling that tightness in his chest. His stomach knotted again as Marcus looked down at him. Harold walked over to the door and closed it, and Brady slid around in his chair to find Harold watching him as he walked back over to where Marcus stood, also looking down at him, giving everything to him.

"What is this?" Brady gestured toward them. "I already told you before. Yeah, I met Cassie about six months ago at the diner. She'd just started working, and I found out she'd just moved here. I didn't ask where she moved from. I already told you that. If you recall, we kind of have our own secrets, so yeah, I don't know anything else. Should I?"

Harold and Marcus were staring down at him.

"Look, I'm not keep anything from you," Marcus said. "At the diner, Tyler said Cassie mentioned Ely, Minnesota, a small town I've never heard of. Jade Arnold's number is from Ely. Let's just say there isn't a chance it's a coincidence, and I don't much believe in them. She's related, family, calling from the place we think Cassie is from. She called six times yesterday, and then Cassie left work. You're sure she never went home?"

He just shook his head, watching the abandoned coffee steaming on the desk, and leaned forward, feeling so damn helpless. "You know when someone has been in your place. I'm telling you, everything was how I left it. I was the last to leave in the morning. I mean, even her uniform from the diner—she always comes home and changes, and she either hangs it up in the closet or dumps it into the dirty clothes hamper. Nothing was moved or out of place. Even the cups in the sink were how I'd left them. She left the diner, and maybe this Jade is with her. Give me the number. I'll call." Brady pulled out his phone.

Harold took the paper from Marcus. "No, I'll give her a call," he said. "You tell Marcus everything you've learned about Cassie from the moment she arrived in town until yesterday."

He could feel this getting to the point where they would tell him what to do, where to sit, how to feel. He finally stood up and held out his hand. "She's my fiancée. I'll call. If this were Suzanne or Charlotte, I couldn't see either of you sitting by and letting someone else call for you. Give me the number, please." He forced politeness into his tone even though his voice had an edge to it, and he just waited.

Harold looked over to Marcus.

"I'm not kidding," Brady said. "This is crazy. Give me the number. I'm calling, and the longer you two stand here and argue about this, the longer it's going to take to find her."

Marcus gestured to Harold, who gave him the number, though he could see he wasn't happy about it. "Do me a favor, Brady," he said. "Put it on speaker so Harold and I can hear. But let's go over a few things first before you call.

Don't get mad. We need to find out who she is, why she called Cassie, and if she knows where Cassie is. Let's start with that, but keep it on speaker so we can hear and we can all have a conversation and talk. And keep it together, Brady. Don't get mad, because we don't know what happened."

He was still standing there when there was a knock on the door. Harold strode over to it and pulled it open, and Colby stood on the other side, holding a sandwich and a bottle of juice. Harold took them both and closed the door, then set them on the desk and said, "Here, Brady."

"Ready?" Marcus said, leaning on the desk. He was still wearing his sheriff's jacket, but he shrugged it off and tossed it over the back of his chair, then gestured for Brady to dial.

He glanced at the number on the paper and dialed, and he heard the ring once, twice. Then there was a click.

"Hello?" It was a woman who answered—a little sleepy, he thought.

"Is this Jade Arnold?" he asked, staring at his cell phone on speaker.

"Who is this?"

"My name is Brady Baker. I'm Cassie Arnold's fiancé. She didn't come home last night, and we're looking for her. We know you called her cell phone several times yesterday. This is Jade, right?"

He felt someone touch his shoulder and looked over to see Marcus in front of him and Harold beside him, gesturing in a circle. He heard a sigh on the other end.

"Brady, right. Cassie mentioned you. I'm sorry. I don't know what to tell you."

"Jade, this is Sheriff Marcus O'Connell. You should know you're on speaker. I'm Brady's brother. We're just trying to locate Cassie. You were the last one to talk to her, from what we can tell, and several witnesses said she was upset after your call. Do you know where Cassie is?"

There was silence. He took in Harold and Marcus, and they stared at his phone and then lifted their gaze to his. Marcus shook his head, taking them both in.

"Jade, how do you know Cassie?" Brady said.

"Look, I haven't spoken to Cassie in a long time. I don't know where she is. Yes, I called her, but that's it. Cassie is my sister."

That had them all really looking at the phone.

"Jade," Marcus said, "although Cassie hasn't been missing that long, we will be filing a missing person's report soon. Is there any place you know of that Cassie would go?"

Harold was leaning in, standing so still. Brady wondered what he could hear in her voice, what he was thinking.

"I don't want any trouble," Jade said. "Cassie didn't say anything to me. We weren't that close. I wish I could help you, but I can't. I'm sorry."

He could feel that she was about to hang up.

Marcus shook his head. "Well, Jade, that's the problem. I don't believe you. Tell me why you called Cassie so many times yesterday and why she was so upset. You grew up in Ely, Minnesota, and Cassie's from there, right? Tell me about that. Is there any other family, anyone else Cassie would call and go see? There has to be other family, a mother, father…"

There was a click, and the line went dead.

"Shit, what the hell was that?" Brady said.

Marcus just shook his head, started to the door, and pulled it open, then called out to Therese.

Harold dragged a hand over his chin. "It seems we hit a nerve or something. First things first. Let's find out who this Jade is, and where, and then I think we'll pay her a little visit. We'll find out what's going on, and then we'll find Cassie."

Marcus strode back into the office and reached for his coat. "Therese has her address in Ely. I've asked her to find out everything she can about her." He pulled on his jacket and gestured to the sandwich. "Come on. I'll take you home."

Brady stared at his brother for a second with a sinking feeling. "You're not going to do anything else? That's it?"

Harold just inclined his head and exchanged a glance with Marcus again as if they knew something Brady didn't.

"No, that's not all," Marcus said, "but you need to go home, and we need to have a talk with this girl. She doesn't want to talk to us, judging by the way she hung up, and that tells me she knows something." Marcus rested a hand on his shoulder. "For all we know, Cassie is at home, but if she isn't, we'll find her." He reached for the sandwich and juice and handed it to him.

"You know I'm not a little kid," Brady said.

His brother nodded. "I know that, but just a reminder, in case you need it: If something happens, you call us— and this is a pretty big something. I'm dropping everything. We're looking for Cassie now, and we'll find out everything, what's going on, and why she didn't come home. Then I suggest you and Cassie sit down and have a heart to heart. Now let's go."

Brady took the sandwich and juice. "Fine, but if you talk to Jade, or with anything you do, I want to be there. I'm not sitting on the sidelines."

His brother let out a sigh, and he wondered if cop Marcus was who he was going to get now. "Agreed, but on one condition, as long as you understand. We're just looking for Cassie now. If at any point this becomes police business, you're taking a back seat."

Then Marcus stepped back, and this time Brady didn't say anything, because whatever was going on, no matter what Marcus said, he was damn sure going to be the first to find out.

"Y ou going to tell him what you found out?" Ryan said to Marcus.

Brady took in everyone who was there in Marcus and Charlotte's kitchen. Charlotte had a fussing Cameron on her hip, but Jenny reached for him, and when Marcus tilted his head to Owen and Luke, one of them had Brady turned and headed into the living room. He felt as if he'd been following orders from one brother and then another all day today.

"Tell me what?" he said. "Someone please tell me what's going on."

He had showered and changed and done another sweep of the now freezing apartment, but still no Cassie. He'd even called her cell phone another dozen times, but each time, it had gone to voicemail. Then he had been dragged over to Marcus's at Owen's insistence.

Frustrating, to say the least. He didn't like this feeling of helplessness.

"Well," Marcus said, "aside from the fact that we've met Cassie and been to the diner where she works, there's no evidence that she exists. The diner has records for Cassie and we have proof of the phone calls from Jade, but Harold did some digging, and we can't find proof that either of the Arnold girls exists other than some cell phones registered in their names. Jade is in Ely, Minnesota, and has a mailing address there, but there is no record of Cassie before six months ago and no trace of her now. She walked out of the diner after work and simply vanished."

Marcus was still in his sheriff's uniform, standing in the living room beside the easy chair Owen sat in.

Charlotte was there too, and she gestured to the duty belt he was still wearing, which Brady knew she insisted he lock up the moment he got home. "Marcus, you can get into this after you put that away," she said, turning to Cameron, who was fussing and reaching for her from where Jenny was holding him.

"Give that boy to me," Ryan teased and reached for his nephew.

Brady could see that Charlotte was about to dig in and make Marcus take a minute to lock up his gun when all he wanted was news as to what the hell had happened to Cassie.

"I know, Charlotte. I will," Marcus said.

"But she does exist," Brady cut in before Marcus and Charlotte could get any more into that husband and wife thing they did. "You met her, and I'm living in her place now, where her things are. She is a living, breathing person."

Luke was sitting on the sofa, Suzanne beside him. He could hear Tessa, Jenny, Alison, and Eva now in the kitchen, and he heard the front door and glanced over to see Karen and Jack, whom he hadn't known were still in town. Harold was the only one not there.

"Marcus is just telling you how it is," Luke said.

"Harold has done some digging too, and he's still checking things out. I made some calls about this mysterious Ely, Minnesota, and that's where things get a little murky. The Jade Arnold who called Cassie's cell phone, who we think is her sister, has a cell registered in Ely, but the town has no record of the two of them. There's no Arnold family there at all. After Marcus filled me in, I took it to my team, because there are too many questions about her. Since Cassie walked out of the diner, out of everyone Harold has talked to, no one has seen her."

"Someone could've taken her," Brady said just as Karen and Jack strode into the living room. Karen wore a slim, long black skirt and bulky sweater, her hair pulled back, and Jack was in a navy knit sweater and blue jeans, something he didn't wear very often.

"Hey, we just heard," Karen said. "Any news?" She had her hand on Brady's shoulder, rubbing it, and Jack stepped over too, Karen though joining Brady where he was now sitting on the big ottoman by the easy chair. "What's this I hear about you wanting to get married, too? We should talk about that."

Jack was resting his hands on the back of the sofa, and for a minute, the way he was looking over to him, he thought maybe this concern had come through him.

"You want to talk about me getting married while my girl's missing?" Brady said.

"Hey, you just turned nineteen and haven't really held a real job or lived yet," Jack said, jumping in. "Gone are the days of getting married super young. But yes, let's table this discussion until after we find Cassie. Then, as soon as she shows, we'll sit down with you and talk about this."

The house phone was ringing from the sofa table at the bottom of the stairs, and Charlotte walked over and picked it up.

"Being up in Missoula, Karen and I haven't checked in with you, so hearing that you proposed to a girl and are playing house after six months is raising a lot of red flags, especially now that she's missing."

He wondered for a moment where this was coming from. Had his brothers also joined in on this discussion? "So is this why you and my sister are still here in Livingston? You came for my birthday, but you're still here. Let me remind you that your life is now in Missoula."

"Brady, Livingston is my home, our home, first," Karen said, correcting herself, and he wasn't sure what to make of the glance that passed between her and Jack. "Jack and I are worried, is all. We still have the condo here, a lease, and a law practice I have to close up now. Jack and I talked last night, and we realized that when we were living here and had you living with us, we could keep better tabs on what you were doing. I kind of feel like I dropped the ball a bit."

"You know what, all of you?" Brady said. "How about we table the talk permanently? I'm an adult, and I get to decide what I want to do with my life, not you. I love her. How about we get back to what Luke found out? You know there could be all kinds of reasons why Cassie Arnold doesn't exist. So what if there's no record? This is a big country. She could be from anywhere. Or is this where you tell me I need to walk away and forget about it, or maybe you'll lie to me? Don't forget, I've been lied to since I was a little kid. I won't allow that again, not ever…" He knew it had come out quite sharply. The way his siblings were looking at him, he felt as if he would be alone in a minute to figure out this situation.

"No one is lying to you, Brady, so get off your high horse about this," Luke said. "We're telling you to get real. This is reality. No one is telling you to forget about her. I know you care, and we know you're serious, and you're right that not one of us can tell you not to feel something for Cassie. God knows each of us has done something at your age that we wish we could go back and undo, but that's not what this is about. Cassie is missing. She didn't come home. She walked out of that diner, and, as of yet, no one has seen her. You're right about one thing: A person can't just vanish into thin air. But I think you need to let Marcus finish, because there's more, way more."

He dragged his gaze over to Marcus, who was standing there, his arms crossed, all cop. "Then what is it?" he said. "What is it you're not saying?"

"I wonder if we should wait for Harold to get here," Marcus said.

Luke hadn't pulled his gaze from Brady, and Owen and Ryan looked puzzled. Suzanne, too. They were looking from one to the other as if none were in the loop.

"No, Harold is going to be a while," Suzanne cut in. "You know that, Marcus. I think Brady is right. You need to just tell us. What's going on?"

Marcus dragged his gaze over to Luke, who only shrugged and then gestured toward him, saying, "Either you tell him or I will, but he needs to know."

Marcus nodded and pulled in a breath. "Yesterday, Cassie received a series of phone calls from Jade Arnold. But Harold went back through her phone records, and there were other mysterious calls in the days before. Two nights ago, a different number kept calling over and over, also from outside Ely, Minnesota. The place boasts a population of just over three thousand, so one random call from there wouldn't raise any flags, but two? The second set of calls came from a man named Perry Warren.

"When Harold was digging, he discovered that a few years back, Ely was rocked by a scandal, a murder at a family cabin. They never found the killer, and it's gone unsolved. The investigation mentioned a family, the Warren family, and questions were asked about their involvement. There were two sisters and a brother, and the body discovered was that of another family member. You see where I'm going?"

Brady was having trouble getting his head around this. So Perry Warren had called Cassie?

Charlotte was standing there now, holding the phone. "Excuse me, Marcus. It's your dad. He wants to talk to Brady."

Marcus gestured to him. "Take the call, Brady. I'm going to change."

But Brady was still stuck on what Marcus had said. Even he had to admit that the questions Marcus was asking had him wondering what the hell was going on. What was Cassie involved in? As Brady reached for the phone and Marcus started up the stairs, he heard his family behind him, talking.

He walked out of the room and pressed the phone to his ear. "Hey, Dad."

"Jake, remember," his dad cut in. "I wanted to wish you a belated happy birthday, but Luke filled me in on this Cassie earlier today. I'm wondering if Iris and I should come back."

Brady was already shaking his head. "No need. Marcus is handling it—though maybe not how I'd like. Let me ask you something, Dad. Remember all the years you had us moving around? How easy is it to just become someone else, use a new name, a new identity?"

There was silence on the other end. Then his dad cleared his throat. "Easier than you might think, but at the same time, you may want to ask yourself, if Cassie isn't who you think she is, could she be hiding something? No one becomes someone else unless she has to."

There it was, the thing he hadn't wanted to admit.

"Then you can find out who she is, who she really is?" Brady said. He could see Alison in the kitchen now with Jenny and Tessa, looking his way.

"I can find out everything, including what she's hiding," Raymond said, "but you may want to ask yourself if you want to know. Do you really?"

He pulled the phone away for a moment and shook his head. "Of course I want to know. If she's in trouble, I want to help."

There was silence again, then, "You may want to think about that a moment, because once you find out a secret about someone, sometimes you wish you could go back and not know. You may not know this yet, but everyone has a dark side, and sometimes there are secrets about a person and her family that you're better off not knowing."

He wondered now whether his dad was talking more about himself or Cassie. "I want to know, so where would I start? What would you do?" He ran his hand over his hair.

"You really want to know what I would do?" his dad said in a way that made Brady wonder whether he would get the truth.

"I want to know what you would do if this were Iris who had disappeared and was in trouble."

There was a sigh on the other end. "If this were me in your shoes, I would go where the questions are and start there."

"So you're saying what, exactly?"

"I'm saying if you really want to know, and you really want to find her, go to Ely. There will be secrets in a small town like that. Take her photo, and take Marcus and Luke. When you start asking questions, just remember that if she was running from something, the girl is scared. So find out what it is she's running from, if it's a person or something she did."

Brady heard the creak on the stairs and turned to see Marcus coming down. "Whatever it is that's going on, I want to know," he said. "I love her, and if she's in trouble, then I'm going to figure out a way to help her."

Brady couldn't help wondering whether Raymond O'Connell was still watching from afar, considering he'd had his eye on his other children all the years he was away raising Brady. How he'd done it, Brady had never really understood. His dad was still a mystery to him, and he realized he really was a different man than he had once thought.

A family of secrets.

Then there was Cassie. His dad was right about one thing: Cassie was hiding something, even considering how little he knew about her.

"You've said very little over there," Marcus said from behind the wheel of Charlotte's Subaru, wearing a long-sleeved green shirt, sleeves rolled up, his coat tossed in the back.

Luke was in the back seat, and Brady wondered whether Marcus had missed the fact that Luke hadn't said one word either since they'd left early that morning on a fourteen-hour drive, on which it seemed Marcus was intent on being the sole driver.

"Okay, what do you want to talk about?" Brady said. Would he ever get used to being part of this family, who seemed to always be in his business?

"Let's talk about Cassie," Marcus said. "Tell me anything about her."

"She has the most amazing smile, and her laugh…when she laughs, it's the most geeky infectious laugh, and she makes me feel alive, and I want to laugh too. She makes me feel good. When I'm with her, I can't imagine being anywhere else, and when I'm not with her, all I'm thinking of is being with her.

"I've been thinking back over the last few days. I've been so wrapped up in myself that I'm trying to think of how I missed this. Was there a problem I couldn't see? As I'm sitting here, thinking about Cassie just up and disappearing, and all the messages I've left, I'm realizing she has to have been getting them, because I've never gotten a warning that her mailbox is full.

"Maybe I'm overthinking it, because what else can I do for all the hours we're on the road, but maybe she has been distracted. I remember something else she said, which I thought was odd at the time. When we were talking about Livingston, she said it seems pretty and perfect, but nothing ever is. I never thought much about that comment until now. You think she was hinting at something then?"

Marcus glanced his way, and Luke, who was in the back, sitting behind Marcus, was watching him too. Luke could read him too well, he realized, in ways Brady wasn't too sure he was comfortable with.

"It seems you've had some time to reflect and think back," Luke said. "The thing is that sometimes when you do that, your head can create a problem where there isn't one, thinking up the kinds of things that make you question whether it's just your imagination. But other times you look back and see things different when you're not wrapped up in your own problems. Maybe you see something she was trying to tell you without really telling you, and you just weren't paying attention. You see it now?"

Brady just stared at Luke, who didn't look away, before pulling his gaze back to the road.

"But I also want to say, young man, that your girl had a secret," Luke continued. "And we know that the best way to keep a secret is to pretend there isn't one. It's sounding to me as if maybe that's what we're walking into. I know we asked you before we left if you really want to know, but…"

"Hey, Luke, don't forget our dad and his secret, which he kept from me, from all of us. So I understand secrets, but everything isn't so black and white. I don't know what happened or why Cassie disappeared, but if the answer to finding Cassie is here in Ely, then I'm not leaving until I find out all of it. Look, I don't have any idea whether she was taken, something happened to her, or she's running from something. But if she's running, I want her to know that it doesn't matter what it is, if she did something or if she didn't. Whatever it is, I want her to know she can tell me, and I'd rather not jump to conclusions, assuming the worst."

Luke didn't pull his gaze, and he offered a nod. "Okay, then we'll find out," was all he added.

It seemed Marcus wasn't too inclined to jump in, as he continued driving the road that stretched for miles, and they all settled back into silence.

They made it to Ely in just under fourteen hours, pulling up to an old two-story house. Brady was in the back, where he'd nodded off, and Luke was now behind the wheel, Marcus in the passenger seat.

"You going to check in with the local sheriff as a courtesy?" Luke asked.

Brady was awake now, looking at the sign on the house, a guest house. The lights were on, and he took in the small town, having to remind himself that it even had residents.

"Not yet," Marcus said, stepping from the car. "I want to get a feel for things first. There's a pub next door. We should grab a bite to eat after we check in."

Luke opened his door, shining the light in the back. Brady grabbed his backpack, into which he'd shoved a change of clothes and his toothbrush. He didn't know why, but he'd also grabbed the ring he'd bought for Cassie.

He followed his brothers up into a place that seemed a hundred years old. The door squeaked behind him, and Marcus was talking to an older man behind an old bar-top counter. Then Marcus held up two keys as he finished filling out a registration card. "Two rooms," he said. "One has two single beds, the other a double."

"I'll take the double," Brady called out, but Luke just ran his hand over his shoulder and ruffled his hair as he pushed him ahead of him.

"Yeah, no. You get a single bed, and it's between me and Marcus who draws the short straw and is bunking with you."

He was about to argue, but it didn't really matter. He followed his brothers to the end of the hall, and Marcus tossed a key to Luke before opening the door across the hall.

"Well, seems I'm bunking with you," Marcus said, dumping his bag on one of the small single beds. He realized there was no bathroom in the room, and as he stepped out, he saw it was across the hall, beside the room Luke was in. Old place, shared bathroom.

"So who picked this place?" he asked, standing in the

hallway and waiting as both Marcus and Luke stepped out and joined him, locking the doors again.

"I did," Luke said. "Does it matter? We're not on a holiday. It's a bed, and there aren't many choices when it comes to finding a place here."

They followed Marcus, who was out the door first, and there was something about the cool night air, which seemed far more humid than home as they headed to the small building next door, a pub and restaurant.

He found himself really looking at this town, wondering what connection Cassie had here. It was one more piece of her that he didn't understand. He followed his brothers into an old pub with a long bar counter, a shelf of hard liquor behind it, and glasses hanging on a rack above. There were a dozen small tables, but no one was there.

They'd just sat down when a man strode over from the back. He appeared to be in his forties, with dark hair and dark eyes, bearded, dressed in blue jeans and a light blue shirt. "You folks passing through?" he said.

"We're actually looking for a bite to eat. The kitchen still open?" Luke asked.

The man glanced over his shoulder and then back to them. "Depending on what you order. The kitchen is closing. Meatloaf special is done for the night, but if you want some burgers, that's easy enough to throw on the grill."

"Burger works for me," Brady said.

Marcus leaned back in his chair, stretching. "Yeah, make it three all around. I'll take a Miller if you have it, too."

Luke gestured in front of him as well. "I'll take a beer too, and bring junior here a soda, root beer."

The man just nodded, his hands on his hips. "Fries all around as a side?"

"Sounds good," Marcus said, and then the man was gone.

Brady took in the atmosphere, the whiskey-colored wood under the lights from the bar, and how empty it was. "Pretty quiet here. Can't see they get much business in a place like this."

Marcus was looking around, just that way of his where he leaned back and looked at everything as if trying to figure it out. "It's a resort town, a lot of lake properties, so they'd likely be busy in the summer but not so much in the off season, which we're coming into."

The man behind the bar carried two beers and a soda on a tray as he walked over to them. "Here's your drinks, and the burgers shouldn't be too long. So where are you folks from?"

Brady reached for his glass, whereas Luke and Marcus both opted to drink from their bottles.

"Livingston," Luke said.

Brady found himself looking over to the man, who didn't seem the type to be working in a place like this. He reminded him a lot of Ryan and Owen, and he didn't know why.

"Montana?" the man said. "That's a ways from here. You passing through or visiting someone in the area?"

Marcus and Luke were looking at each other across the table, and Brady wondered why they weren't questioning this guy.

"We're looking for someone, actually," he started before he felt Luke's foot connect with his shin. "Ow!"

Luke glanced at him. "Sorry about that, kid," he said —though, somehow, Brady didn't think he was.

"You know anything about the Warren place and what happened there?" Marcus asked, and Brady found himself staring at his brother, wondering why he had jumped right to that.

"Everyone around here knows about the Warren place. It's on the lake, just north of town. Kind of rocked the community. That kind of thing doesn't happen around here. Gets crazy in the summer with folks from the city and stuff, but it was the old man who was found dead, murdered, shot with a shotgun. No idea who did it. I know they looked at the kids, but nothing turned up.

"He had trouble with all of them at one time. The wife, we heard, ran off before that. Some say it could've been her sneaking back into town, angry over something, or just getting even. But that's just talk, you know. The kids were a handful for him. I know the police were investigating what trouble one of them might have brought around. He was a good guy, didn't deserve it. That's the kind of big-city trouble we don't want here."

Brady was squeezing his glass, feeling the cold from the ice as he stared up to a man who seemed to be a wealth of information. "So they had no evidence at the scene and no idea who did it? You mentioned kids. How many were there?"

The man crossed his arms now, staring down at them. "Just the three of them, Perry, Cassie, and Jade."

He could hear a ringing in his ears, and it seemed everything stood still as he heard the names. A coincidence? He remembered what Marcus had said: There was no such thing. For a moment, though the man was still talking, he didn't hear anything.

"I don't think they ever caught up with those kids after questioning them the first time," the man said. "There was talk that they did it, but no one could prove anything. They had an airtight alibi, and no one ever found the gun. But then, Ralph Warren would never have won father of the year. Some said he was too hard on the girls, and some say he took them on when no one else would. Depends on who you talk to. So who did you say you were, again?"

"Marcus O'Connell," Marcus said. "These are my brothers. I'm actually a sheriff in Livingston. You mentioned Ralph Warren took the kids on?"

The man stared at each of them and then over to Marcus. "Sheriff…well, welcome. Yeah, the kids weren't his. Lea, his wife, they were hers. They came with her. Ralph always said they were walking trouble, especially the girls. No, he had some folks' sympathy. Not many men would take on someone else's kids. You have an interest in Ralph Warren? Are you investigating his murder and what happened?"

What was it about listening to this man that gave Brady more questions than answers? "No, we're looking for Cassie," he said. "You seen her?"

Both Marcus and Luke glanced his way. Right, he wasn't supposed to be talking, but then again, this was his girl.

"Cassie…" The man made a face and shook his head. "Can't say I have, but if I see her, I'll let you know."

What was it about the way the man said it? When he walked away, Marcus and Luke both sat up and leaned on the table, giving everything to him.

"Well, I'd say that's interesting, except now I've got a whole lot more questions than before," Marcus said in a low voice.

"Yeah," Luke said. "What do you say, after we eat, we find out where this Warren place is and take a drive out there?" He leaned back and glanced over to the door, then back to him.

"In the dark, at night?" Brady said.

Luke glanced Marcus's way only once. "Can't think of a better time."

"Yeah, we'll see if anyone's there," Marcus said.

"And if no one is?" Brady asked.

Luke lifted his beer, unsmiling. "Then I guess we'll have a look around, see what kinds of secrets are out there."

"And what if there's nothing at all?" Brady asked.

Marcus lifted his beer. "There's always something," he said. "Sometimes, you just need a place to start."

Then the man strode out of the back, carrying three plates. Even though he was sick with worry over Cassie, Brady realized they were one step closer now to getting some idea of what had happened to her.

B rady waited by the back door of the Subaru as Marcus tossed the keys to Luke and rested his hand on the roof of the car. The sense of urgency that tightened in his stomach and across his chest had him fighting the urge to yell and scream at his brothers, at the night. He couldn't remember ever having felt so helpless.

"You know what? Before we head out to the Warren place, I want to have a word with the owner of the guest house," Marcus said. "Just give me a minute. You know people in small towns can be a wealth of useful gossip." He tapped the roof and zipped up his brown sheriff's jacket before starting to the guest house.

"Whatever that is about, I'm not waiting out here," Brady said, and he didn't have to look back to know Luke was right on his heels. "This is my girl. In case you missed that fact, whatever you and Marcus are thinking of doing or asking, don't leave me out of it. I'm not some little kid, and I'm tired of being treated that way."

He felt a hand on his shoulder as he was about to start up the steps. Luke pulled him back and turned him.

"You're tired and stressed and worried, so I'll let it go, but Marcus and I being here with you, we're not keeping things from you," Luke said. "This is what we do. Understand, Brady, we're not sneaking around behind your back; we're helping you. That's why we're here, and that goes back to you being family. Every one of us has been in a spot where we've needed one another. We've had this talk, remember? The skills Marcus and I have are different, and we don't go around questioning each other. Marcus is doing what he's good at, and that's getting answers for you. So before you go storming in there, all hot-headed, saying something you can't take back and making it so we don't get the kinds of answers we need to find Cassie, just shut it. Stop, already," Luke said, then stopped talking, letting his meaning set in.

"Fine, I get it, and I'm not ungrateful, but hear me when I say I'm tired of feeling as if you and Marcus know more than me and are the only ones who can find Cassie. Granted, I'm not a sheriff or in the special forces like you, and I don't have experience doing this kind of thing, but I can think for myself. I'm not a total idiot, and I'm not going to sit by on the sidelines and do nothing while you and Marcus do everything. I want to be there to hear what's being said about Cassie, what's being asked about her. You have any idea how I'm feeling right now, not knowing where she is, if something happened to her, if we're even in the right place? For all I know, someone took her, or something happened to her, and she's back in Livingston, yet here we are."

Luke rested a hand on his shoulder. It was dark out, and in the light of the single bulb outside, he could just make out his brother's expression. "I know, and I hear you. Just so you know, we don't expect you to sit on the sidelines, but let Marcus do the asking, and just listen, okay?" Luke patted his shoulder.

He wasn't sure why he felt as if he'd just been scolded. Instead of answering, he pulled open the door and stepped inside, Luke behind him, seeing the small entryway.

Marcus was standing over at the counter, talking with the man who'd checked them in, who had glasses and white hair and was nodding. They both headed over, and Marcus gestured to them.

"These are my brothers, Brady and Luke," he said. "This is TJ. He owns the guest house, and his son Jarrod, next door, owns the pub. It's a family business. TJ was just filling me in about the Warren place."

Brady kept his hands tucked in his pockets as Marcus turned back to the older man, who smiled and gave a nod in hello.

"So no one has lived out there again, no one from the family?" Marcus asked.

TJ only shrugged. "No. They couldn't, I think. They had some state investigators come in, and the local chief questioned the kids and neighbors, too. It was messy, the scene. The Warrens were always the center of talk. They were a bunch who never really fit in. Ralph was a retired cop, a deputy. He held the peace, but that's about all he did. You either had trouble with him or you didn't. Then he met Lea—a nice woman, it seemed. She kept to herself. Then there were the kids…"

"She had three kids, right? Jade, Cassie, and Perry?" Marcus asked.

TJ was taking in Marcus, everything about him. The sheriff's jacket, he thought, was what had the man talking. "No, no, Lea had only the two girls, Cassie and Jade. Jade was the youngest. Perry wasn't hers. I think folks kind of confused that part of it, mainly because he showed up at the same time as Lea and the girls. Perry was Ralph's kid from a former girlfriend, I think was the talk, but he showed up the same time Ralph met Lea. Ralph said from day one that the girls were a handful, fourteen and fifteen. He was having trouble keeping them in line, he said. Walking trouble is what he called them, and they were looking for all kinds of trouble with boys and anything else, too. Not the brightest, he said. He expected one of them would get pregnant, drop out of school, not amount to anything. Then there was Perry. Old Ralph said Lea wasn't much of a mother, and that was where her daughters got it from…but the way he talked about her sometimes, you wondered what went on and why he kept her there instead of showing her the door. If it were me, I'd have sent her packing."

Just listening to the man left him with a sick feeling.

"So for how long was he married?" Marcus said. "Your son next door said Lea left him and her kids."

TJ wasn't smiling and lifted his hand. "They weren't married, though I think some folks thought they were. I remember Ralph saying one day that she'd just left, left him at his lowest. He'd been laid up for a bit, shot on the job, then never returned to work because of an injury. Was drinking, we heard. He figured she'd run off with some lowlife. The only good thing she did for her kids was leaving, but at the same time, he said those girls didn't have much going for them up here and all." He gestured to his head.

Brady had to fight the urge to set him straight, and maybe that was why Luke moved over closer beside him.

"So you're investigating the murder," TJ said. "Is the case going to be opened again? Because I know a lot of folks around here were really uneasy about it. I'd sleep better at night knowing they've caught someone. But then, there's a lot of speculation and questions around the kids, rumors that one of them did it. Never found the shotgun that killed him, and the kids…nothing could be proven. Not sure why. Then again, no one heard much from the kids after, either."

Brady pulled out his cell phone and held it up. "Is this Cassie?" He took a step closer, holding the photo up, him and Cassie, a selfie he'd taken on the sofa in her living room. Her smile was infectious, but her eyes, he thought now, as he looked, had a sadness to them. Why hadn't he seen it before?

"Could be," TJ said. "So you and Cassie are together? She's a pretty thing."

Brady was still holding up the phone to him, seeing that the man had stopped smiling.

"Yeah, she has those doe eyes just like her sister. I can see why Ralph warned people about her. She's a looker for sure, trouble…"

Brady squeezed his phone, having to fight the urge to snarl. "She's my fiancée, and she has a good heart, kind. We're looking for her. So what about Perry and Jade? When was the last time you saw them?"

The man frowned and shook his head, and for a moment, Brady thought he'd hit a nerve. TJ gestured to the phone Brady was still holding up, and he pulled it away, taking in her photo and again fighting his anger at the way Cassie had been trash-talked. If she'd left this, grown up with this, no wonder she didn't want to talk about it.

"Well, I don't personally know the girl, only what I heard, so I would have to take your word for it," TJ said. "As far as Perry, he works for old Rashim, who owns the wreckers. He lives in a trailer on the property. Heard he was fighting the probate on the house or something, as

Ralph died without a will, and it seems the courts and stuff are dragging it along, seeing if any other next of kin come out of the woodwork. Don't think there will be much left if it's ever settled."

Luke angled his head, and there was an exchange between him and Marcus. "So you're saying no one lives out at the Warren place, and it's been empty ever since he was killed? What about Jade? Have you seen her?"

The man seemed to consider something. "Not sure. You may want to check with Perry, but as far as the girls, they all but disappeared after Ralph was killed. Some say they went looking for their mama—a lost cause there, if you ask me. Ralph always said she didn't have much going for her. Called her a dingbat, stupid." The man tapped his head again.

Luke put his hand across Brady's chest and somehow had him turned. "Higher road, Brady," he said to him at the door, then pushed him along outside.

Marcus was following, and they somehow had him walking down the steps when the only thing he wanted to do was go back in and make that guy take back every nasty, sexist, dirty, cruel, mean thing he'd said and thought about Cassie and her mother, even though he didn't know her. It just seemed so wrong.

"Why in the hell didn't you say something to that jerk?" Brady said. "The way he talked about Cassie, her mom, her sister… Seriously, how can you be so calm about it?" He knew he was loud, and Marcus had the rear car door open for him. Luke was already behind the wheel as Marcus rested his arm on the open door, waiting for Brady to get in.

"I'm not calm, not by a longshot, but what would it have accomplished if I got angry at that man? What could I have done—tried to change the mind of a man who has some pretty stagnant ideas of women? Remember, we're trying to find Cassie, not win a popularity contest. For the record, I've heard that kind of talk about women before. It happens too often, especially from a generation that has no respect for women and degrades them. How to take the higher road is something I've had to learn along the way. We want to find Cassie. Fighting bigots like that isn't something I want to give any energy to right now. Besides, we have a lead: the brother, Perry. Let's find the wreckers and go pay him a visit."

"You think we'll find Cassie there?" Brady said. Maybe Marcus was right, but he still wanted to go back in and set that man straight, because then he'd feel as if he'd done something.

"I think it's a start," Marcus said. "Remember, Perry called Cassie too, so let's find out from him what's going on. Just maybe, he knows exactly where Cassie is."

The wreckers was a typical graveyard of vehicles surrounded by a metal fence and padlocked gate. The yard was floodlit, and there were lights on in a building ahead, but there was no way to get in. Marcus stepped out of the running car and pulled at the chain and lock, peering through the gate.

"What is he doing?" Brady asked.

Luke chuckled from behind the wheel and looked back at him. "What he's good at: finding a way in."

"The gate is locked. What, is he going to climb the fence…?" Brady said—but he stopped when that was exactly what Marcus did, jumping down on the other side.

"Any other questions, young one?" Luke said. "Have some faith in your brothers. You know, we do know a thing or two about how to find people, and Marcus always did know how to get into places that wanted to keep people out."

He watched as Marcus walked into the wreckers until he couldn't see him anymore. He remembered now what Marcus had said the night of his birthday, which seemed a lifetime ago but had been only a few days. His brother had been in trouble, on the wrong side of the law. He was seeing Marcus now in a way he hadn't before. He had the kind of experience that could help him understand that life of crime and the guys he chased after as a cop better than anyone else could.

"So what do we do, just wait here?"

Luke didn't look back at first, then turned off the car as Marcus reappeared, accompanied by a man in a black wool hat and heavy coat, shorter than him. The man unlocked the gate.

"Nope," Luke said, already halfway out of the car. "Let's go in and have a talk with this Perry, or would you like to stay here and keep warm?"

Brady realized his brother was messing with him as he stepped out and followed him over to the now open gate, where Marcus was talking with the older man.

"This is Rashim," Marcus said. "He owns the place. Perry lives in a small RV out back."

Brady walked through the gate and waited. Whatever Marcus then said to the man had him pulling the gate closed but leaving the open padlock on the fence and walking back the other way.

"Let's go," Marcus said. "Rashim said Perry's home. He's here every night. Rashim was just about to leave. Scared him, I think, walking in the way I did. He thought he was in trouble when he saw my sheriff's jacket."

"You didn't tell him you're not local?" Luke said.

Marcus laughed under his breath. "No. We're in, right? Or would you rather have waited until morning when they're open? Not sure I want to be away from family any longer—or bunking with Brady, who will likely keep me up all night moping because we haven't found Cassie." Marcus nudged him as they walked.

This was definitely a side of his brothers he hadn't known. He just shook his head as they walked around the building, past a pile of old cars, smelling the metal and rubber and something old and burnt. A small older trailer came into view, with a canopy out and lights on inside. Two chairs were set up outside the trailer beside what looked like an old barbecue, as well.

Luke was first to the trailer, looking around, and then he knocked on the door. Brady could hear footsteps, and then the door opened to reveal a man with shoulder-length dark hair and a beard in a gray wool sweater for work in cold weather.

"Yes, who are you?" the man said.

"Are you Perry Warren?" Marcus asked.

The man stared at Marcus, taking in his sheriff's jacket. For a moment, he said nothing, and Brady could feel his unease. He wasn't sure whether the man would run or do something.

"Look, I'm looking for Cassie," he cut in. "I'm her fiancé."

The man dragged his gaze over to him, then took in both Marcus and Luke, then stepped out of the trailer and closed the door. He was tall, about their height, and slender, in his early twenties, maybe.

"Yeah, I'm Perry. Who are you?"

He hadn't answered about Cassie, he realized. From the way he was standing there, looking at him, Brady realized there was no resemblance between the two.

"I'm Brady Baker, and these are my brothers, Marcus and Luke O'Connell. We're looking for Cassie. We know you called her, and she's missing now."

Marcus reached over and tapped his chest, maybe to get him to stop talking.

Perry wasn't giving too much away, as he pulled his

arms across his chest as if considering what to say. "I didn't know she was getting married. She never said anything."

What the hell was he supposed to say to that?

"You know Cassie is missing, and we're trying to find her," Marcus said. "A series of calls came in two days ago from Jade and then, prior to that, from your number. We heard from the diner where Cassie works that the calls from Jade upset her. She left the diner after work, and she hasn't been seen since. You know anything about that?"

Brady wasn't sure if it was surprise or shock in the man's expression. He said nothing as he stared at Marcus. Then he bolted past Brady, pushing him back so he hit the ground.

"Dammit! I hate it when they run," Marcus yelled.

Luke was running after him, and Marcus too, as Brady hurried to his feet and gave chase. Luke was fast, tackling Perry and taking him down, and then Marcus was there. Brady was already out of breath by the time he caught up to where Luke had Perry pinned to the ground, his arms up high behind him.

"Get off me! I didn't do anything," Perry yelled.

Luke just looked up to Marcus, keeping his knee in Perry's back and his arm pinned up.

Marcus knelt down to him. "Then why did you run? Come on, get up," he snapped and grabbed his arm. Luke grabbed the other, helping him up. "Are you going to run again? Because if you do, I'll cuff you and call the local sheriff so he can join the discussion. Or you could just talk to us and tell us what the hell is going on. Why'd you call Cassie? Why'd you run? Does this have anything to do with Ralph Warren's murder? And what about Cassie—is she involved somehow?"

Perry was breathing heavy, and he shook off Marcus and Luke. Brady could tell he really didn't want to say much. "You a cop investigating this, or are you just looking for Cassie?" he said.

Brady stepped around his brothers so Perry had to look at him. "This is about Cassie," he said. "I love that girl. We're getting married, so please, please, if you know where she is, tell me. I don't care if she's in trouble, or you, or whatever it is. I just want to find her and make sure she's okay."

He fisted his hands at his sides, feeling the cold. Luke and Marcus flanked Perry, likely expecting him to run again. He was seeing the wisdom of having his brothers there.

"Cassie is not missing," Perry said. "I just saw her. You say you're looking for her, but you're not here as a cop?" He dragged his gaze over to Marcus and gestured to the sheriff's jacket and logo.

"I'm the sheriff in Livingston, Montana," Marcus said. "I'm here for my brother. Cassie is his girl, so this is family business. So you've seen her? She's here?"

Perry dragged his gaze from Marcus to Luke and back to Brady. "Yeah, she's here."

Brady's knees weakened.

"Like here, staying with you, or here in Ely?" Luke said. "And why the secrecy? Why'd she take off? You still haven't answered us about the calls and what's going on. There seem to be a whole bunch of secrets, and we'd very much like some answers."

Perry was shaking his head. "Well, if you want answers, you're going to have to talk to Cassie. You said you're family, but I don't know you. For all I know, you're the old man reaching up from the grave one last time."

Brady wasn't sure what to make of that statement. He had a sick feeling that there was so much more going on than they knew. "Look, if you don't want to tell us where Cassie is, then get her on the phone. Let me talk to her."

Perry dragged his gaze back over to him and then turned. He took a step away before looking back. "Well, come on. You want to talk to Cassie, my phone's in the trailer. But that's it. You talk to her and then you leave, because that's all I'm giving you."

As Perry started walking back to his trailer, Brady glanced to Luke, who fell in behind him, and then Marcus, who shrugged and joined them.

"We'll get Cassie on the phone and talk to her, get her to tell you where she is," Marcus said. "But I'm telling you, Brady, there's something going on here, and I'm not liking it. There are always secrets in a small town, and I'd bet my bottom dollar these kids know something about Ralph Warren's murder. They either know something or did something."

All Brady could do was pull in a breath and glance away. "You know what, Marcus? I just want to hear her voice, that's all. I want to know she's okay. Before you jump to the worst-case scenario, tying her to a murder, I want to talk to her about what happened, why she took off. At the same time, with family secrets, we have our own, don't we?"

Marcus shook his head and glanced away, swearing under his breath. "You have a point, but I want to make sure you're not walking into something that could pose a serious problem for you. Because the deeper we get into this, instead of more answers, I've got only more questions."

It was dark, cold, and far too quiet.

The dirt road, not much of one, looked to be taking them nowhere, and the bushes were overgrown in places, but Luke seemed to know exactly where he was going. A few cottages and houses had been built around the lake, but he had no idea how many homes were out here. It was a mix of summer places and homes people lived in all year, he thought. Luke pulled into a driveway up to a small darkened place bordering the lake, more a cabin than a house.

Brady couldn't get her voice from his head. He shut his eyes, remembering how Perry had called her and he'd stood there like a fool in the dirt with three pairs of eyes on him, not knowing what to say to the girl he loved, who'd run off on him without a word and wouldn't pick up the phone because he was calling.

"So you sure this is it?" he asked.

Luke turned off the car. In the driveway beside them was a tarp-covered utility trailer. He wondered how much different the place would look in the light of day.

"This is it, the place owned by Ralph Warren. You said Cassie would be here," Luke said and looked back, and so did Marcus.

For a second, he had to remind himself to breathe as he thought of all the questions he'd wanted to shout at her when she'd said only, "I'm sorry."

"She said she'd be here."

That had been all he was able to get out of her on the phone when he turned his back on Perry and his brothers. She wouldn't take his calls, but she'd take Perry's? It hurt, and he'd been furious. He'd had to remind himself that seeing her face to face was the only way to get answers, so he'd found a way to bite out, "Tell me where you are. I'll come right now."

He pulled in another breath. That short conversation played over and over in his mind as Luke and Marcus waited for him to say something else. All he did was push open the door and step out of the car, and his brothers followed.

He listened to the crickets, the sounds of a country night. It reminded him of a place he'd stayed with Raymond when he was ten, someplace in the Midwest—the Ozarks, maybe. They'd stayed for three months. There'd been a dock and a small boat.

He started to the cottage, seeing a screened-in porch. Everything was dark, and then he heard something.

"Cassie?" he called out, taking another step on the path around the front of the house.

A flashlight flicked on, and there was just something about her as she lifted the flashlight so he could see her face. She was in a dark coat with fur lining around the hood. He couldn't have explained to anyone the relief and the anger that hit him at the same time.

"How did you find me?" she said.

Of all the things to ask, that was the one he hadn't expected. He didn't have to turn to know that Luke and Marcus were lingering in the background, yet they hadn't said anything.

"You know my brothers, Marcus and Luke," he said. "You went missing. You didn't answer my calls. I thought the worst. Of course we've been looking for you. You think I would just let you walk out of my life like that? Why? Why did you do it? What happened? I mean, Cassie, come on. I ask you to marry me, and you just disappear? I thought something happened to you. Do you have any idea how worried I was? Marcus got into your phone records, found out who called you and from where, so we went looking for you. Now here you are without one word to me about what's going on. Are you in trouble?"

She was just standing there, about a foot between them, and he took another step to stand right in front of her. He realized her cheeks were wet. She was crying.

"Talk to me, Cassie. What's going on?"

She was shaking her head. "I never thought it would catch up to me, Brady. You know, I thought I could walk away and have a fresh start. I deserved that. I didn't want to come back to this place. I tried to forget. I hate this place."

"Well, why are you back here? Is it because of what happened to Ralph Warren?"

Cassie stilled, and her breath caught. "How do you know about that?" Her voice was low and trembling, and he thought he heard a kind of fear.

"Looking for you and putting the pieces together," he said. "In town at the pub, and at the guest house we're staying at, people filled us in on what happened, but my brothers started digging, and things turned up—small-town secrets and lies, an unsolved murder, and a whole lot of talk. You still haven't answered me, Cassie. You can tell me anything, you know."

She flicked off the flashlight, but it didn't matter, since they were so close. He reached for her hand and took it from her, and she pulled back and nodded. "It's not as you think or may have heard."

"Then tell me how it is and why you're here," he said. Even he could hear the demand in his voice. "Would you have called me? Would you have come back?"

She glanced away to the house. "It's cold out here. Let's go in, and I'll start a fire," she said.

He wasn't sure whether she'd answer them inside, either, but she started around the house, and he followed her up the steps, his brothers behind him.

She pulled open the screen door and stepped inside, then flicked on the lights. He could see his breath as he took in the small kitchen and living room with a woodstove. She opened it to reveal kindling and paper, and cut wood, too, as if it had been ready and waiting for someone to start a fire.

He heard the door close and turned to see Marcus and Luke in the dim light as Cassie struck a match and lit the kindling, and after a moment, he listened to the wood crackle. She closed the woodstove and stood up, swiping her hands together, and then tucked back her dark hair. Her curls appeared even more out of control now, and she lifted her gaze and smiled, revealing her dimples, but he still saw tears in her eyes.

He knew this was her way of trying to make a tense situation bearable. He found himself taking in the old kitchen, the yellow cupboards, and the dry goods on the shelf. The floor was hardwood, with an old dated sofa and easy chair in the corner and a big boxy TV on the floor that likely weighed more than three hundred pounds. He wondered what era it was from.

"Cassie, Luke and I can step outside if you want to talk alone with Brady," Marcus said.

She lifted her gaze to Brady and then over to his brothers behind him. "I thought I could move away and start again. I changed my name to my mother's maiden name, Arnold. Then Perry called and told me I had to come home." She shook her head and looked up. "Home… This is a place I never thought of as home. Ralph Warren treated my mother like shit."

Marcus leaned against the counter, crossing his arms, and Luke said nothing.

Cassie was looking right at Brady now. "We asked her to leave, told her we had to leave—but we had Perry to think of. Ralph treated his son like shit, too. He liked to lift his hand to us, giving a smack across the face or the back of the head if you talked back at all. He liked to hit our mom, yet we couldn't report him. You know why." She was looking right at Marcus. "Because he was a cop. Who would we have told?"

Marcus shook his head. "We heard he was a cop, a deputy here, before some injury in the line of duty ended his career."

Cassie looked over to Marcus and then back to Brady, her smile gone. "Line of duty… I love the spin, as if he was some hero. He was no hero. He wasn't shot in the line of duty. He was a bad cop. He pulled a gun on a man he had trouble with, and the guy shot him, likely in self-defense. Took out his knee. Ralph shot him dead in return. He bragged about it to my mom when he was drinking. He carried a gun around, slept with one. He scared all of us, and my mom said she couldn't leave because he'd find her, and she was terrified of what he'd do."

"But we heard your mom did leave, and you stayed?" Brady said.

Cassie furrowed her brows and shook her head. "Mom didn't leave by choice. She was right about one thing: He would never have let her go. Being a cop, he could find her anywhere. He wasn't the man she first met, but then, I don't think that man ever existed."

She crossed her arms and then dropped them and unzipped her coat, one he didn't recognize. She was wearing blue jeans and a red floral shirt that he didn't think was hers, either.

"What do you mean, your mom didn't leave by choice?" Luke asked.

Cassie was looking down at the ground. When she lifted her gaze, her eyes were darker and seemed to flicker with something he hadn't seen before.

"Cassie, do you know where your mom is?" Marcus said.

She looked over to Marcus and then back to Brady, then pulled in a breath, jutted her chin to the door, and said, "She's out back."

Marcus looked out, and Luke put a hand on the door to open it, but Cassie was shaking her head.

"She's not waiting out there," she said—and there was something about her expression, something that gave him an awful sick feeling when she swallowed as if her mouth were dry. "She's buried out there."

Lights were on in a few places around the lake, Brady could see from where he stood at the shore, the reflection of the moon disappearing as it slipped behind some clouds. He heard the screen door slap closed, then footsteps through the debris of fallen leaves.

It was pitch dark now, and his ears stung from the cold, his breath fogging in front of him. He dragged his gaze over to Cassie, who was walking with Marcus by an old well surrounded by a few barren trees, which had dropped all their leaves.

He felt a hand on his shoulder.

"You okay?" Luke asked.

Brady just glanced to his brother, then back to the cottage, seeing the smoke from the stove drift up. Cassie had walked out of the house, right past him, without a word. He should've been over with her, but instead she'd just walked away, and he'd let her.

"Yeah, I'm just…"

His brother patted his shoulder again. "I know. It's a lot to take in," was all he said. He seemed to be waiting for

Brady to figure out that he needed to walk over to Cassie and do something.

He started walking, one foot in front of the other, his hands in his pockets. He wasn't sure what Marcus was saying as he knelt down, looking up to Cassie, but whatever it was, she nodded.

He walked right over to her, slid his arm around her, and pulled her against him. "You should have told me."

Marcus was running his hands over the ground, clearing the leaves. He wondered if this was his brother or a cop who'd just heard about a crime. What would he do?

"I never planned on telling anyone, Brady."

"So what happened, Cassie? Who did this?" Marcus asked, looking up to her from where he squatted.

Brady could feel her tremble, and he wasn't sure if it was from the cold. She glanced over to Luke, who walked around Marcus, just looking at everything: the ground, the trees, and farther behind them. There was a small dark cabin next door that he could just make out, a summer place that seemed relatively deserted.

"I came home one day, and my mom was dead, lying on the floor in the kitchen, with blood from a head wound. Ralph said she fell and hit her head, but I know it was a lie. Jade was there. She was hysterical when I walked in. She said they were fighting again, or rather, Ralph was trash-talking our mom, telling her she was useless, stupid, that no one else would put up with her crazy talk, that she couldn't even put together a decent meal and everyone in town knew she wasn't quite right in the head…that a dog was more useful than her."

Cassie squeezed her fists in front of her. She hadn't pulled away, and she looked up to Brady now. Her face was pinched, with no more forced smile. "It was always the same. I'd heard it all so many times. I knew the kinds of things that came out of his mouth, anything to bring her down so his foot was on top of her. And my mom just took it, every cruel remark. Jade said she didn't see what he'd done, but she'd heard the slap, the commotion. It's a sound you just don't forget. She covered her head with a pillow, and when she heard the shouts and knew something was wrong, she went out there into the kitchen. Perry was there, too, and Ralph was doing CPR. That was how I found them. Then he just stopped, and it was the way he said it—cold, no emotion, so matter of fact, as if he were talking about the weather. 'Well, that's that. She's dead.'

"Ralph just stood there, looking down at her. Before that, I had never thought I could hate him more, but I was wrong—and in that moment, I was furious with my mother, too, because if she'd had the courage to walk out the door, she wouldn't have been lying there, dead."

She went to step away, and he let her. He could see, even in the dark of night, that this was a side of Cassie he'd never been able to put his finger on, a side she'd been hiding. What was it about feeling someone's heart break wide open? She suddenly seemed so raw and real. She'd hidden something like this, and he'd had no idea.

"You didn't call the police?" Brady said.

She dragged her gaze over to him, a spark of anger directed his way. "I was seventeen, and he was a cop. Are you new to the world and unsure on how things work?"

She glared at him as if he could never understand that the kind of privilege Ralph was born to would never extend to her. He shook his head.

"Who would I call?" she continued. "It would always have come back on me. He was the law, and I was nothing. You think anyone would have listened? The townspeople always saw us one way, and we knew Ralph was responsible for that. He talked, and people listened. We didn't have a voice, and he did. He planned it well. He made sure we would never be believed."

"So who buried your mom?" Marcus cut in, likely because this was just a bad situation and Brady was clearly in over his head. What would Marcus do, considering he was the sheriff in another town, another state? There were so many secrets and lies in Ely, and he figured they'd only scratched the surface. There was way more to come, and he knew Cassie still had more to share.

"Ralph made Perry dig the hole, and he told Jade to grab a sheet and wrap her body. Then he made Jade and me carry her out. He stood there, telling us to dump her body in the ground, and then he watched as he made us fill in the hole, the entire time telling us we couldn't tell anyone, that it was my mom's fault. It was an accident, he said. She'd hit her head. But if we told anyone, he'd make sure it came back on us. Perry, Jade, and me, we had to listen to him. He said he could do it, and we believed him."

Marcus finally stood up, reached into his pocket, and pulled out a wool hat to pull over his head. Yeah, it was cold. Marcus let out a sigh, and he wondered if he would reach for his cell phone and make the kind of call that could see Cassie arrested, being led away by some cop.

"So who killed Ralph? Which one of you shot him?" Marcus said.

Brady just stared at his brother in horror, because that was quite a leap. Cassie pulled her arms across her chest and said nothing.

"Cassie?" Brady finally prompted, stepping closer to her, and rested his hand on her shoulder. "Look, no one would blame you."

She shook her head. How did one go on, living under the same roof as a monster like that? She looked over to him. "I'm not a killer, Brady, but Ralph was. I don't think he had an ounce of remorse in him. He went on as if nothing had happened. He was still a cop. He told people she ran off. I was standing there the first time he said it, staring at him in horror, wanting to scream 'Liar!' But I knew I couldn't. The rumors started. I wanted to leave, but I was in school, and so were Jade and Perry. We talked about running, but then what? We had nothing, and Ralph had already said that if we talked, ever, he'd find us and bury us right next to our mom.

"And you know what? I believed him. He was a cop, and he had friends, reach, access to databases. He could make sure we would never be able to really disappear and be free of him. Law enforcement agencies all work together and share information. He could put out an alert, a warrant, and get us hunted on some trumped-up charge. It was something he would and could have done.

"I lived here for a few years, and every time he walked through the door, my stomach was so twisted up in knots that there were days I would puke. I slept in fits because you never knew when he would be there. I woke up once, and he was in the bedroom Jade and I shared, sitting in a chair, cleaning his gun in the middle of the night. He didn't have to say anything. He had so many guns locked up, and every week he would clean one and then another.

"Then he was shot. For a moment, I was so happy, because the other deputies showed up and told us as if we were some loving, close family. Then I learned it was just his leg, his knee. He would live, but he was no longer a cop. It was a disability, apparently a word cops don't want to hear."

Brady was staring at her, then dragged his gaze to Marcus, who must have known he was looking his way. He didn't think he'd ever seen the grim look he was seeing now on his brother's face.

"There are some bad cops out there, Cassie, that's for sure," Marcus said. "Unfortunately, the system isn't perfect. Ralph was the kind of man who should never have been allowed to have a gun. I'm sorry for what you've been through, and you're right. You wouldn't have been believed."

He thought he heard Luke swear as he glanced away, his hands now shoved in his pockets.

"You know," Cassie said, "when I showed up in Livingston, I was truly happy for the first time in my life. I didn't have to worry about living under the roof of a monster who controlled everything." She let out a sigh, then was looking right up to him, and he wanted to put his arm around her again. "I had never thought it could get worse, Brady. But it did. When he came home from the hospital, he was always there. I remember standing there, making soup for all of us in the kitchen. He would tell us to get him something, make him something, do something. He held up the shotgun he was cleaning, pointed it right at me, and pulled the trigger.

"There was a click, and I swear it went right through me. It was empty, but for a minute, I didn't know. Your brain can't tell the difference. I jumped and wet my pants, standing there in a mess on the floor. I knew if he saw, he'd lose it. He just laughed over my reaction and said it wasn't loaded, and then he walked away—with that limp, the cane, because his knee was gone.

"He put the gun away, and I cleaned up, but I knew there was no way I could live like that anymore, because one of us would end up dead. Jade was younger than me, and I suddenly realized I had to do something, especially when I saw the way he was looking at her. It's just that look a man gets in his eyes, and you know a girl isn't safe. Jade was only sixteen, and he was a grown man. I told

Perry, I warned Jade, I said no one was coming to help us…"

Brady stood in horror, and his brothers said nothing, though he knew Marcus understood what she was saying. The sick feeling that had been there suddenly changed. He'd never really considered this before. It was something that happened to other people, no one he knew. Until now.

There was a siren outside, then another. He could hear them. Marcus looked up. The only one who didn't seem shocked was Cassie, as she pulled in a breath and then let it out, just looking straight ahead as if she'd expected it.

"Perry called me and told me to come back," she said. "The chief here was asking too many questions about Ralph, and his alibi had fallen through. Jade was supposed to disappear. She used the Arnold name like me, but she came back, because she said Perry was going to be arrested. The chief believed it was one of us who had done it. I don't think he much cared which one. Jade said he'd get us all on conspiracy. They pulled her in and interrogated her for hours…"

Marcus took a step around him, and Luke too. He looked up, seeing lights as two cop cars pulled in front of the house, around the Subaru, the sirens whirring. Cassie took a step closer to him and another until she was standing right in front of him, and Marcus, he realized, was walking out to the cops, who were now getting out of their cars, shouting out for Cassie. Luke jogged after Marcus, holding up his hands.

"Cassie, what the hell is this?" Brady said.

"I tried running and starting fresh, but I couldn't let Perry and Jade go down for something I did. I decided time was up. I'm sorry, Brady. I love you, I really love you, and the thought of marrying you, although it scared the hell out of me…we'd have been good together."

He slid his hands over her cheeks and pulled her closer, resting his head against hers, her hands fisted in his jacket. "What did you do, Cassie?"

He didn't have to look over to know the cops were coming their way—shouting, flashlights shining on the ground, footsteps.

She pressed a kiss to him and pulled back. "I called the chief before you showed up here. I confessed to shooting Ralph, said it was me and only me, and Jade and Perry knew nothing about it."

Then the cops were there, two of them. They pulled her from him roughly and pushed him back, then turned her around, and she nearly stumbled as they pulled her hands behind her back and mirandized her.

"You understand these rights as they've been read to you?" one cop said, and Brady could hear the anger.

"Ouch, not so hard!" Cassie cried out as one slapped cuffs on her. They were far from gentle, and he could see this was personal to them.

"Hey, stop! What are you doing?" he yelled. He was furious.

Marcus was there suddenly, reaching over, and pulled him back, not about to let him race over and save her. "Stay out of it, Brady! Cassie, you say nothing to them, you hear?" he called out.

Luke was talking with one of the other cops as Cassie was led away. One of the cops had a thick mustache, but it was dark out, and he couldn't really make out anything more, just a coat and a badge.

"Don't you hurt her," Luke said. "I can see well that you're angry there, boys, but I don't want a scratch on her."

Brady went to dart around Marcus, but he grabbed his arm.

"No! You have no choice here, Brady," Marcus said, squeezing his shoulder. "You interfere, and they'll charge you. It'll only make it worse for her, and then you won't be able to help her."

"Where are you taking her?" Brady finally demanded. "Can't you do something, Marcus?"

"She's a cop killer," one of the deputies called back. Another cop was walking their way.

"Right now, they're going to book her," Marcus said. "I can't do anything. They're going to interview us now, because the only thing they want to do is close this case. She confessed and called them. I already told them I'm a sheriff in Livingston, but I have no jurisdiction here. We'll figure it out, but she called them and said she killed Ralph."

Some distance away, Luke was holding his hands up in defense as if he was already going at it with the other cop.

"After what he did?" Brady said. "He killed their mom. He was a monster."

Marcus was standing right in front of him. "And Cassie was right. She won't be believed. It comes down to her word against the word of someone who wears a badge."

He just stared at his brother, then dragged his gaze back to the cop cars, their lights still flashing, seeing Cassie being put in back and wishing he could get her out of there and hide her.

"So you're saying she doesn't have a chance," he said.

The one cop who'd approached Luke and had been talking to him was now walking their way, likely to question them too and find anything, one more nail to seal Cassie's coffin.

Brady took in Marcus, who stared long and hard at him, and he only nodded, because he'd be damned if he gave them anything that would hurt his girl.

He dragged his hand over his face as he sat on a hard bench against the wall in the St. Louis County Jail. The lights were bright, and the butterflies in his stomach had dark sharp edges that kept ripping him from the inside out, reminding him of the time he'd watched his father die. It had been one of the worst days of his life next to this one.

Raymond wasn't dead, but just the same, the memory still haunted him. It had been the worst thing he'd lived through before feeling that horrible, awful feeling that Cassie was going to be lost to him forever. This was cruel.

He still couldn't believe she'd called the police, said she'd killed the man who had murdered her mother and tormented her and her siblings.

Why hadn't she come to him and just told him everything?

Who did that, confessing to the police? He stared over at Marcus, who was talking to one of the cops who had been at the cabin and arrested Cassie. He was a big man in a navy jacket with a thick mustache, the man who'd tossed over his shoulder that his girl was nothing more than a cop killer.

Cassie was not a cop killer!

He felt the tap on his leg as Luke sat down beside him. "You okay there?"

What was he supposed to say to that?

"Uh, are you kidding?" Brady said. "What about Cassie? How do we get her out?"

Luke was leaning forward, resting his arms on his legs and shaking his head. "It may not be that simple. Just trying to get in to see her is proving to be a monumental task. Not much cooperation here." Luke dragged his gaze over to Marcus and then back the other way to the counter, where cops stood behind a wire mesh, old and dated. "Marcus is trying, but they don't seem too cooperative at this point, even with a sheriff. They want the case closed, end of story. We don't know what Cassie has said…"

"Excuse me, are you Brady?"

He looked up to see a girl with short dark hair, the same wavy texture as Cassie's. He could see the resemblance. She wore blue jeans and a striped shirt under an orange coat, and Perry was with her. He found himself slowly standing to see these siblings, wondering what hand they had played in this.

"You have to be Jade," was all he said. He felt Luke's hand on his arm.

She nodded, her eyes big. "Cassie told me about you, and Perry called me and said you were here. Have you seen Cassie? The police called us and said they arrested her. She really called them and said she did it?"

Perry glanced past him, keeping an eye on the other cop, who was talking to Marcus.

"But you know more, don't you?" Brady said. "She didn't do it, did she?"

Jade opened her mouth to say something, but Perry put a hand on her shoulder, and she must have understood, as she just shook her head.

"Brady," Marcus called.

He dragged his gaze over to his brother, who gestured to him and was walking his way. He hesitated only a second before stepping away from Cassie's siblings, and he couldn't explain what he was feeling, knowing she was drowning and they'd pulled in the line that could save her. Luke was still there, too, and he turned away as Marcus closed the distance, glancing past him.

"They agreed to let you see Cassie," Marcus said. "Just remember, though, when you go in, be careful what you say, because they'll be recording everything."

There was only a second of relief as he pulled in a breath and took in the warning, then nodded.

Marcus glanced behind him again, staring at the siblings. "Who is that with Perry?" he asked, his hand still on Brady's shoulder. "Is that…?"

"Jade, yeah, her sister," he said. "But I don't think they're here to help her."

A grim expression filled Marcus's face.

"What are the chances of getting Cassie out?" he asked.

Marcus only shook his head. "Less than zero, unless there's a miracle. She confessed to killing a cop, and I'm betting there was never a report of domestic abuse. Him being a cop, her accusation isn't going to hold up at all. But we're working on it, making calls. Go talk to Cassie, but remember what I said."

Marcus gestured over to the cop who was waiting, and Brady started walking, one foot in front of the other. He stopped in front of the cop who hated Cassie, he knew, because of what he believed she'd done. From the pissed-off glare in his dark eyes against his light skin, and his thick dark mustache, he wondered if the man ever smiled.

"We're giving you only fifteen minutes as a courtesy to your brother," the man said.

Brady didn't think it was much of a courtesy, but he reminded himself not to push it, so he said nothing as he followed the man into the jail and through a door, where he was led into a room.

There was a small window with bars and mesh, and the walls were gray, and there was a table and two chairs. He realized this was the first time he'd been in a jail. He heard the heavy door, the clang of keys, and there was Cassie, her wrists still cuffed behind her back. The cop who had led her in closed the door and stood right there.

Her eyes reached out to him, and he realized the cop intended to stay, to listen, to intrude.

"Please uncuff her and give us a minute. She's my fiancée," Brady said, hoping for some decency.

The man looked over to Cassie, then stepped out, leaving her uncomfortable and cuffed.

When the door closed, Brady walked right over to her and put his arms around her, pulling her closer, and hugged her tight. "Are you okay?" he said and stepped back, taking in his girl, who seemed stripped right down.

All she did was nod, but it was rather shaky and forced.

"Why did you call and tell them you did it?" His voice was low. He found himself looking around, wondering how they would be listening. "Did you ever tell anyone what he did to you, that he killed your mother, how he hurt her and stalked you and your sister? Did you tell them what he would've done?"

She was shaking her head, though he already knew she

hadn't. He just had this feeling that she'd toss herself under a bus to protect someone she loved.

"So who really shot him? Because I don't believe for one second you did it."

She hesitated and shook her head. "Brady, it doesn't matter."

"It does matter, Cassie. As you said, you were good in Livingston. There was no reason for you to go back, but you did it for Jade, for Perry. They wanted you back to, what, take the fall for them? I don't get it. Why?"

"One of us was going down for it…"

He heard the key and the door, and two cops walked in, including the one with the mustache. He wanted to remind these assholes that he'd been there only a few minutes, but the cop walked right over to Cassie and took off her cuffs.

"Well, it's your lucky night," the cop said. "The shotgun was recovered at the wreckers in your brother's trailer. Detectives are talking to Perry now. He made it easy, showing up here, saying you confessed for him. It seems you're free to go while we sort this out."

"What? No…" Cassie started, but Brady slid his hand around her arm.

"So the charges are dropped against Cassie?" Brady cut in to stop her from doing something that would have her cuffed again and locked back in a cell. He could feel how worked up she was.

The cop slid his gaze over to her and then back to Brady. There was no friendliness there when he stepped back and said, "For now."

Brady wasn't sure what that meant, but he reached for Cassie's hand and said, "Let's get out of here," then started out of the room.

"Brady, we can't leave," she said. "I don't know what's going on, but…"

He had her hand. "Cassie, let's not talk here. We'll figure it out, but not here."

They stopped at the counter, where a cop had set down her coat and an envelope with some personal items in it. He reached for her coat and helped her on with it, and she took the envelope and signed something for her things, then followed him out the door.

His hand was on her arm, and he spotted his brothers and Jade. Marcus was shaking his head and started walking over to him, while Cassie pulled her hand from his and raced over to Jade, then hugged her. Luke and Marcus gave him an odd look and gestured to the door.

"Time to go," was all Luke said.

Brady wasn't sure how Marcus managed it, but he somehow had Jade walking ahead of them with Luke, out the door, down the steps. They were already at the Subaru, which was halfway down the parking lot. Brady was so out of the loop as to what had happened, and he reached for Cassie's hand and stopped her on the sidewalk outside the jail.

It was so late. He should've been tired, but he had so many things to say to her.

"Just wait up a second," he said. He was still holding her hand, and he wasn't sure what to make of her expression as she looked up at him. "You didn't shoot him, did you?"

She pulled in a breath and then another and glanced away, but this time, he reached over and touched her chin and made her look at him.

"This is me, Cassie," he said. "I love you. You can tell me anything. Please… This is a shitty thing that happened to you, and if he wasn't dead, after what he did to you, I'd kill him myself. Whoever did it deserves a damn medal."

Her brows furrowed. She seemed confused, as if she didn't think he'd believe her or stand beside her. He really did have so much to learn about her.

"It was my idea," she said.

"I asked you if you shot him. Cassie, I love you. We're getting married. You need to share things with me. No lies, no secrets. Come on."

She ran her tongue over her lips and seemed to consider something. "I couldn't pull the trigger. He laughed at me because he knew I was a coward, and he called me a stupid bitch just like my mother. Then Perry took the shotgun from my hands and pulled the trigger while he was still laughing at me…" She shut her eyes.

He knew the memory haunted her. He lifted his hand to her face. "We'll get him off. Karen and Jack are lawyers, and damn good ones, too. But no more secrets, Cassie. You have to tell me everything. If you're scared, or something happens…" He gestured toward her, then turned to his brothers, who were waiting.

When he pulled his gaze back to Cassie, she was looking up to him. She stepped closer, sliding her hands over his face, and then lifted her lips and kissed him before pulling back. He just hugged her and held her for another second.

"How did I get so lucky to find you?" she said.

He slid his arm around her and pulled her closer, then pressed a kiss to the top of her head as he started walking with her again. "I'd say we're both lucky."

She lifted her gaze, looking up to him, leaning her head against his shoulder. Those dimples popped, and that smile he hadn't thought he'd see again so soon appeared. "Okay, no more secrets," she said.

He glanced over to his brothers. Right, no more secrets —but his father was the one secret he still couldn't talk about. There are always secrets and lies in a small town.

"I love you, Cassie," he said before he kissed her again.

"I love you, Brady." She leaned into him.

Maybe, someday, he could tell her.

"I can't go around making crimes go away," Marcus said, sitting on the small single bed at the guest house in Ely, untying his boots. "I actually have to uphold the law. What you're asking is something I can't do." He pulled off his boots and dumped them on the dated hardwood floor, then untucked his dark shirt with a beer logo on it from the waistband of his jeans.

"The kid isn't asking you to make a crime go away," Luke said. "He's asking you to do something so his girl isn't railroaded again. This kind of thing seems to happen in our family, and you well know how the situation could get twisted so Cassie suddenly finds herself cuffed and behind bars again. We just witnessed a miracle, but if the police come knocking a second time, she won't be so lucky."

Brady dragged his gaze to the door to the adjoining room, where he had left Cassie to rest on the double bed they would share that night. The walls were thin. She was exhausted, and this family of hers was mixed up in something not that different from his own family's drama.

"No one is asking you to break the law, Marcus,"

Luke continued. "But if you didn't notice, Cassie was ready to be a martyr and fall on her sword because she believed the cops were coming after Perry and Jade. Those kids are in over their heads. Then, by some miracle, they found the shotgun at Perry's…" Luke lifted his hands in the air.

Brady was too tired to speak, so he just sat in the vinyl chair and listened to the back and forth between his brothers. With his military background, Luke picked up on things, understanding the way the world worked. Suddenly, Brady's overtired brain realized what his brother was saying.

"Wait, how did they find the shotgun?" he said. "It turns up all of a sudden…"

Marcus leaned back on the bed, which creaked, and plumped two pillows behind him. He groaned as he shut his eyes, tucking his hands behind his head. "Who says it wasn't planted?" He opened his eyes and looked right at Brady, then Luke. "It was way too coincidental. Cassie was in jail, behind bars. She had confessed and called the cops to come and get her, and then, all of a sudden, they find the shotgun they couldn't before. I mean, I do this for a living. Evidence doesn't show up unless someone wants it to."

The door creaked, and they all turned to see Cassie standing there, barefoot in blue jeans and a striped T-shirt, her dark hair a mess, appearing as tired as he felt. Marcus didn't sit up but didn't look away, either, whereas Luke stood from his chair and gestured to it. Cassie just shook her head and leaned in the doorway.

"I thought you were sleeping," Brady said.

She glanced his way, then looked over to Luke and Marcus. "Couldn't. Every time I shut my eyes, my mind started racing, and then I heard you talking. You're right about the shotgun. I don't understand how it suddenly turned up."

Marcus was looking right at her. He sat up, letting out a sigh. "Who had the shotgun, Cassie?"

Cassie firmed her lips, and for a moment, Brady didn't think she'd answer.

"Cassie, I already told Luke and Marcus that Perry was the one who pulled the trigger," he said.

"Even though it was my idea?" she snapped, crossing her arms under her breasts. He wondered whether she was cold or just stressed and tense.

"Cassie, you had every right to want to do what you did," Marcus said. "I can't even begin to understand what you were feeling. Because of who Ralph was, you didn't think you had a choice. I'm a man, a white man, and even though I like to say I understand, I'm not a girl, and I can't imagine being preyed upon like that, being that vulnerable. I can't pretend to understand how helpless you thought you were, so much so that your only option to be free of a man like that was to kill him. Could you have called the police?"

Brady looked at his brother, wondering whether he really understood that she hadn't had a choice. Marcus was still staring at her, then dragged his gaze over to him.

"You heard what happened, what he did," Brady said, feeling as if he had to defend her. "He killed her mother, and then he was going after her sister. What choice did she have?"

He felt a hand on his shoulder, Cassie's hand, and saw her long, slender pale fingers. He touched them, gripped them, and saw the way she firmed her lips. He couldn't figure out why she wasn't angry.

"I don't think that's what Marcus is saying, is it?" she said.

Marcus just pulled in a breath and rested his hand on his knee, looking over to her. "The thing is that questions will be asked, Cassie. I don't mean to sound insensitive, but you're not going to get any sympathy. I'm telling you this straight up, as that's the only way to deal with this. From the conversation I had with the chief here and the little I picked up on, Ralph Warren was a cop, one of theirs, and any accusations about him now will be seen as a way to get the murder charges dropped. With the killing of a cop, that's something that doesn't happen.

"I understand that you couldn't go to the police because they worked with him, and it wouldn't have been investigated. You would basically have been shut down, and it would have come back on you way worse. But you know that already." Marcus circled his hand. "They won't accept anything now, any claims that he was abusive, because none of you said anything at the time. Even if he was a problem with other cops, you're not going to get them to admit it, and our chances of finding any reports of abuse anywhere else are pretty slim, too, because there were no incident reports, no calls from you, from your mom, from Jade or Perry…

"It's a shithole cycle where you have nowhere to go for help in a small town—but, and I hate to say this, it would have been a fight for you even in a big city, and you likely wouldn't have seen any help, because he was part of the system. I'm thinking, Cassie, it would be best if you and Brady went back to Livingston now. I already called Karen and Jack for some help here, and I filled them in. Sorry I didn't ask you, Cassie, but, as Brady has pointed out, you two getting married kind of makes you family, and we look after our family. I do think we should tell them about your mother and where she's buried. Then there's Perry. But it all starts with that shotgun. Who had it? Who knew where it was?"

Brady wasn't sure Cassie was going to answer. He reached for her hand. "Cassie, come on, who?"

She pulled in a breath. "We all knew where it was, hidden in plain sight at Ralph's place. We buried it where my mom is." She sighed. "Someone would've had to dig it up. Perry wouldn't do something like that…" She pulled her hand away and then walked back into the other room without saying another word. Luke and Marcus exchanged a look, and Brady got up.

"I'm going to…" He gestured after her.

Marcus just lifted his hand in acknowledgement, and Brady stepped into the other room and took in Cassie, curled up on the double bed.

He pulled the door closed, walked over to her, and climbed on the bed behind her, pulling her against him. He pressed a kiss to the back of her head, and her hand went over his, which he slid over her stomach, holding her.

"You think Jade did it?" he said.

She turned and faced him, so close to him. "Yeah, but I'm having a hard time understanding why she would do it. That's all I've been thinking, lying in here. When we dropped her off at home, her apartment, I didn't think anything of it. Our alibi for that night was an old boyfriend of hers, and she lives with him now. He covered for her, for us, but he was recently picked up for possession. Perry said he talked, that he told the cops about us to get himself out of trouble.

"Then Jade started calling. I told them both no at first, said I couldn't come back, but then I had no choice, because Jade was pulled in and questioned, and she said they were asking about me, as well. She was freaking out. We agreed we'd stick together. You know conspiracy carries quite a sentence, and they told her they were coming after all of us. She was scared. She's always been scared. I just didn't think she'd throw Perry under the bus. But the gun… Only the three of us knew it was there."

He tucked her hair behind her ears. "You said it was your idea to kill him, but Perry shot him. Was Jade there?" he asked. Her eyes had always flickered with mischief, but he could see the weight of what she carried now.

"She was—but it was my idea, Brady. Perry only did what I couldn't. He shouldn't be in jail. That's why I called and confessed, because it was me, and there was no point in all of us being arrested."

What was he supposed to say to that?

There was a tap on the door, and they both sat up on the bed.

"Yeah?" he called out.

Luke stepped inside the room. "Marcus just talked to Jack. He's reached out to a friend of his who's coming down to help your brother out. Jack and Karen are also on their way. Cassie, I know you didn't say anything about your mom, but it's time. You need this to go away. Both Jack and Karen agree that you need to show them where your mom's body is. If you can prove that Ralph killed her and buried her, there's a chance they can make all of this go away. It won't be easy, but listen to them."

Cassie glanced back to him, and he wasn't sure she was going to agree. Luke stepped back out of the room, maybe to give them time to talk. Brady took in the backpack he had tossed on the chair, and he slid off the bed. Cassie suddenly appeared so sad.

When he unzipped the bag and pulled out the ring box, she was looking at him but said nothing. He stood in front of her and opened it.

"It's not much," he said, "but I bought it and wanted to

give it to you the day you disappeared. I asked you to marry me…" He pulled it out of the box and reached for her hand, then slid it on her finger. "It was all I could afford."

She rested her hand on her lap, then lifted it and shook her head. "It's perfect, Brady…but with all this, I just don't know if we should. I could still very much be in trouble, and you may well consider walking away. You didn't sign up for this."

He sat beside her on the bed. "I signed up for you. And my family was right: They're here for you. Have some faith, because Karen and Jack are good. They'll do what they can, and so will Marcus and Luke. No one is going to throw you under the bus."

She looked over to him and nodded. "You know I really love you, Brady."

He reached for her, pulled her close, and kissed her. "I love you, Cassie. Just remember, one foot in front of the other, okay?"

She kissed him again and then pulled back, and he wasn't sure what she was thinking about when she said, "You're lucky to have a family like you do."

"We're lucky," he said, "because when we get married, they'll be your family, too."

CHAPTER
Eighteen

There was so much snow on the sidewalk as Brady pulled up in front of a two-story craftsman and parked behind the sheriff's car that had scared the hell out of Cassie the first time she'd seen it. As he shoved the vehicle in park, she had to remind herself that she was okay.

She'd tried to wrap her head around the fact that Jade had told her boyfriend about the gun, and the redneck loser had dug it up and added it to his stash. He had a business selling pills, and when he was busted, he'd tossed out the information that Jade, Cassie, and Perry had killed Ralph Warren.

That was the only reason shit had hit the fan and they'd suddenly come under suspicion in a cold case that could've stayed dead and buried. He'd planted the shotgun at Perry's soon after. Her sister had trusted a man who was the scum of the earth.

"You okay over there?" Brady said. "You've said hardly anything since we got home."

He was so damn good looking, dark haired, and that

smile of his… Sometimes she couldn't believe she'd been lucky enough to meet him.

"You mean home to a freezing apartment with no heat?"

"We should look for another place," he said.

She knew he was right, but at the same time, the apartment had been a welcome sight after the days they'd spent away. "What kind of debt do I owe Karen and Jack and your brothers? They got Perry out of jail and on probation, and we got to give my mom a proper burial. I still can't believe there will be no charges against me. I didn't really believe I would walk away unscathed."

Then there was her relationship with her sister, who'd trusted the wrong man with the kind of information she should've taken to her grave. She knew Jade felt horrible, and she wondered if Perry would forgive her.

"You don't owe a debt, Cassie," Brady said. "You're family. This is what we do. We have each other's backs. If one of us is in a jam, we all come, we all help out. We never turn our backs on family."

She slid her hand around his wrist and took in the tiny ring she wore. She wondered if he would ever get that it meant more to her than anything. "I like your family, Brady."

He glanced past her and jutted his chin out her window, and she turned to see a middle-aged man step out of the house with a woman who had short dark hair and a beautiful smile, who lifted her hand in a wave.

"Who's that?" she asked and looked back to Brady.

A smile touched his lips, and he leaned in and kissed her, then said, "Someone I want you to meet. That would be more family."

The man and woman smiled out to him and waved again.

"Come on," he said.

He pulled open his door, and she followed him out and waited for him to walk around the front of the vehicle to join her on the sidewalk. He linked their fingers as they walked up the steps to the house.

"Cassie, this is Iris O'Connell," he said, then leaned in, kissed Iris's cheek, and hugged her.

"Oh, Brady, I missed you," Iris said. When he stepped back, she took Cassie's hand, then rubbed her arm. "Cassie, it's so nice to meet you. I've heard so much about you."

"You, too. Thank you," was all Cassie could get out. She looked over at the man beside Iris, who had such deep blue eyes. His hand was on Brady's shoulder.

"And, Cassie, this is Jake," Brady said. "He's Iris's partner and kind of like a dad to me."

Jake and Brady seemed close, she thought. She could see what he meant.

"Jake, Iris, it's nice to meet you," she said. "I'm Cassie, Brady's girlfriend."

Brady reached for her hand and lifted it. "I think you mean to say fiancée," he said, then pulled her closer and kissed her.

She was ushered inside the house, hearing the voices of his family, and, for the first time, she felt she was part of something bigger.

Turn the page for a sneak peek of
THE STALKER coming next in THE O'CONNELLS
Available in print, eBook & Audio

What's coming next in The
O'Connells

A small-town girl who's a bit of a misfit. The perfect guy who's anything but. Will his suspicious behavior reveal things she doesn't want to know?

Dark secrets are resurrected in this new O'Connell novel.

Alison Sweetgrass-O'Connell believes she's forever a misfit and will never fit in.

After struggling to recover from a teenage crush that dealt her a crippling blow, Alison watches from the sidelines in the small town of Livingston, Montana, which hasn't been friendly to her. Silently, she believes everyone's seemingly perfect lives have a dark side. And soon her beliefs prove true.

Alison meets young, attractive med student Bennett Warren, new to Livingston. Suddenly, Bennett is showing up everywhere she is—and then, in her good fortune, he turns out to have rented the apartment right next door.

At first, she's convinced it's fate, and maybe there is hope for her, but a suspicious turn of events has her fearing she's being stalked by someone who knows one of her secrets, something no one should know.
She tries telling herself she's imagining things, but she soon realizes someone has been inside her apartment, going through her very personal belongings. She finds herself looking over her shoulder, not knowing who she can trust. When she confides in Bennett, she's convinced he thinks she's crazy, too.

Then Alison comes across evidence that has her questioning not only her sanity but also the real reason Bennett showed up in Livingston—and even more disturbing is the possibility that him moving right next door to her wasn't entirely coincidental.

The Stalker

CHAPTER 1

Did anyone else slip out of bed in the morning planning to kill someone?

As Alison stared at the list of names in her journal, she underlined Belinda Lee's again in red, picturing her perfect smile, perfect body. Belinda wrapped every guy around her finger, and every one of them had believed everything she'd said. She'd thrown Alison under the bus with lies and more lies to save her own skin.

It seemed her entire life had been a series of people believing she was an easy target, a scapegoat who would never fight back.

Her pen hovered over the page again. She had to remind herself that Cassie Arnold—scratch that, Cassie Baker—shouldn't be on the list. She crossed out her name and then circled the two columns, which contained the names of everyone who had hurt her with lies and stories, targeting her just because of who she was: someone who could never fit in.

But Cassie had never done that. Her only crime had been falling in love with Brady.

There was a knock at her bedroom door, and she closed the red hardcover book and shoved it in her bedside table just as the door opened. There was her dad, Ryan. She wondered whether she would still feel like she did now, as if life was against her, if she'd been raised by him instead of Wren, a man who'd loved her but hated her mother.

He had been twisted, sick—likely why she was the freak she struggled not to be today.

"You could wait until I say to come in, you know," she told him, wondering if sarcasm and nastiness dripped from her voice.

Her dad raised a brow, and then there was a tug at his lips. Of course, he was fighting some amusement at her expense. "Then you'd never answer," he said. "Figured you were either sleeping or ignoring the world. I see it's the latter. Everything okay, kiddo?"

There it was, the fatherly concern she had to remind herself was normal. He lingered in the doorway, his hand on the frame, dressed in his ranger uniform, already packing his gun.

"Fine," she said. "Why wouldn't it be?"

Oh, maybe the fact that she was still stuck in her misery since seeing Belinda Lee just the day before. She had walked into the Bluebird, the bustling restaurant Alison had worked her ass off at for the past year, doing all the shit jobs to try to get the coveted evening waitress position, where the tips were high and the hourly pay was a dollar more. Belinda had walked in and landed the job after just five minutes with the manager. It had been just one more kick to the head.

"I thought you and I could snag breakfast together this morning and talk and catch up," Ryan said. "Your mom is across the street with Charlotte. The two of them are working on Marcus's campaign."

Right, her uncle was running to keep his job as sheriff. It seemed her dad was ready to poke his nose into her business.

"I'm not really hungry," she said. "I have work." *In six hours.*

Her dad angled his head and stared at her with those deep O'Connell blue eyes. He seemed at times to know what she was thinking and feeling. But maybe that was just her imagination. He didn't move or look away, though.

"Pretty sure you work the dinner shift," he said. "It was a big deal last week when you no longer had to work the breakfast and lunch crowd for a pittance, as you put it, of tips. You're in the big leagues now. Or has something changed? Are you back working the early shift?" He crossed his arms as he leaned against the doorframe with seemingly no intention of walking away.

She tried to figure out what to say. She didn't much like being caught in a lie, and she wished her grandma were around to talk to and just make her feel better. But she was just someone else who had left her.

"Fine," Alison said. "But I'm not ready to eat breakfast. It's too early."

"Nonsense," Ryan said. "Get dressed. Breakfast is the most important meal of the day." He gestured toward her as he took a step past the doorway. She knew she was frowning, but he didn't seem to notice. "We haven't had much time to talk, and it's time to check in, since you haven't been around for family night this week. If left to your own devices and given space, you'd continue to be stuck in your head, miserable, gathering enough rope to hang yourself, as I can see from your face now." He glanced to his watch and then back to her. "Say, ten minutes, downstairs. I'll warm the truck."

"What? Wait, you mean we're going out?" Now she was sitting straight up, alarm tightening her chest. She was wearing a baggy nightshirt on her messy bed, and her image in the dresser mirror revealed bed hair and unwashed makeup from the night before.

"Yeah, breakfast out," he said. "You have time. We'll talk, catch up, and you can tell me everything that's going on in that head of yours. Namely, you can explain why I'm hearing second-hand that you applied for an apartment rental at the Carlyle and didn't bother saying anything to your mom and me. So come on, get up, and clean up and get dressed. You have ten minutes. See you downstairs." Then her dad tapped the door frame and was gone, walking away.

She listened to the creak on the stairs, a sinking feeling in her stomach as she said, under her breath, "Shit."

"Yeah, I heard that," Ryan called out. "Ten minutes, Alison. Get your butt in gear."

She wondered now how much more he was listening to when she thought he wasn't. As she climbed from bed, she was stuck on one question: How had he found out about her applying to rent an apartment? She hadn't told anyone when she spotted the for-rent sign, called the number, and filled out an application that didn't include her parents' names for references, yet he seemed to know even though she had yet to hear back from the building manager about whether her application had been approved.

Right, just one more person who was messing with her.

"You know there's no shortage of restaurants," she said. "Did you have to bring me to the place I work?"

At least they were in a corner. She fought the urge to run her fingers through her wet hair, which was still damp from the quick shower she'd grabbed. She'd thrown on white sweatpants and a matching bulky and comfortable hoodie, and when she'd finally gone downstairs, her dad had been standing at the bottom, checking his watch.

"Hey, stop complaining, considering I'm the one who had to wait for you," Ryan said. "When I said ten minutes, I didn't mean for you to take a twenty-minute shower and then try on everything in your room while I waited downstairs. I thought you'd throw something on, brush your teeth, wash your face, and we'd go."

Alison reached for a packet of sugar and tapped it before ripping it open to pour into the steaming coffee Nan had brought as soon as they sat down. Nan was the waitress who had trained her, an older woman close to retirement, with hair she'd let go pure white and a smile that always warmed her. She'd reminded Alison that customers liked a happy waitress, not one with a chip on her shoulder. She stirred in the sugar and then tapped her spoon on the edge of her mug, fighting the urge to roll her shoulders, very aware that her boss, Chad Hargrave—older, married, and balding—was walking their way.

"It wasn't twenty minutes," she said. "I'm not a guy, who can get out of bed and throw on the first thing he sees. I'm a girl. It takes me more than ten minutes to get ready."

She didn't have to look up to know that Chad was now standing there, but she lifted her mug to drink as she took in the man who had welcomed Belinda with open arms.

"Hey there, Alison," Chad said. "Listen, we're kind of short staffed, so I need you to start earlier today. Then I'm going to put you back on the lunch shift for the rest of the week. Okay?" He patted her back and smiled at her dad, then didn't wait for a response before walking away.

She felt her jaw slacken, her appetite disappearing, and she squeezed the handle of her mug, firming her lips, wondering how that had just happened.

"Why didn't you speak up?" Ryan said.

She dragged her gaze back to her dad, who lifted his mug, took a swallow of coffee, and then closed up the laminate menu and slid it to the edge of the table.

"And say what, no?" She could feel her attitude with a dash of anger. Why did she feel as if there was a "Kick me" sign taped to her back?

"Well, for starters, didn't you say the dinner shift is what you wanted?" Ryan said. "You make more tips there, but now you're suddenly working a shift you don't want again. When you work for someone, you don't have a lot of say, but you do have a voice. If you don't speak up, you'll get walked over. So is this a permanent demotion? Just saying, you have to use your words and talk and communicate instead of going right to that place of having a chip on your shoulder and being angry at the world."

She rested her elbows on the table, holding her coffee mug between both hands. Nan was running plates out from the back, wearing blue jeans and a faded blue shirt. The breakfast and lunch crowd were casual, but for the dinner shift, they were a little more on the dressy side.

"I don't have a chip on my shoulder, but he's my boss," Alison said. "I'm pretty sure if I said no, the next thing he'd say is 'Pick up your check. You're fired.'"

She wasn't sure what to make of the amusement in her dad's expression as he shook his head and said, "Now you're being overdramatic. Words matter, and you have to speak up. Talking isn't your strong suit, I know. You hold things in, Alison. You get pissed off and think the world is out to get you, but it isn't. What you give out is what you get back. Well, at least you can show up for family night now, and we can keep tabs on you again, check in and find out what you're doing, talk…you know, like families do. And maybe you can explain why you're suddenly renting an apartment and moving out."

She took a swallow of the bitter coffee that needed something else, more sugar, maybe cream. She put the mug down on the table. "It's called being an adult. It's time to have my own life and place. I didn't know I'd been approved to rent the apartment. I applied and was told they'd get back to me. So how did you find out?"

She wondered for a moment if her dad would answer her question. He glanced over to the side as Nan hurried past and said, "I'll be right back to take your order!"

Ryan pulled in a breath and leaned back, nodding. "Being eighteen doesn't make you an adult," he said. "There aren't many people I don't know in this town, and since you didn't put any references down on your application, my phone was suddenly ringing. I went to school with Trish Huckman, who manages the Carlyle. She was wondering why you signed the application as Alison Sweetgrass, not O'Connell. Everyone in this town knows you're my daughter, but you're still using Wren's last name? I don't like the kinds of questions that raises. As you know, people create problems that aren't there. They come up with their own version of the truth."

She had hesitated, since she usually wrote Sweetgrass-O'Connell. She had even wondered, for a moment, if he'd understand.

"A habit, I guess," she replied. "I didn't think it was a big deal."

She stared at her coffee. Sometimes letting a lie roll off

her tongue was easier than explaining why she did the things she did. When she flicked her gaze back to her dad, he was staring at her and leaning back, and his blue eyes held an edge of hurt. Okay, now she felt like shit.

"It is a big deal, Alison," he said. "You're my daughter…" He let out a sigh, and she knew he was taking it personally. "Alison Sweetgrass-O'Connell is your name. You're an O'Connell. Or do you have a problem with being my daughter? I thought we were past this."

She didn't know what to say. She wished she could go back and undo that moment and write her full name. Wren hadn't exactly been father of the year, yet she was still holding on to that piece of him even though she would never walk away from her family here.

"No, Dad, there isn't. You're being ridiculous. It was just a blip and meant nothing. I wasn't thinking…"

She stopped talking. His gaze lingered with that dark look she knew well. It was just who he was. She never knew when he'd call her out, but she didn't think he'd let this slide.

"Okay, the truth?" she said. "I wanted anonymity, to do this myself and not have it get back to you or Uncle Marcus or anyone in the family. But, apparently, I can't even do that right. So everyone knows about me. Not sure how I like that."

She thought of Trish, the woman who'd shown her the one-bedroom apartment, and felt another knife in her back.

Her dad didn't say anything for a second. Then he pulled in a breath. "This town knows about all of us. We've been in the spotlight for too long, and it seems everyone knows how to connect the dots between us. Trish wanted a reference. Since you've never rented a place before, it makes people nervous. I vouched for you.

You've got the place if you want it, but why the rush? You're just starting out, just finished high school. You have your own room in a roomy house, and you're just starting to put money away. It's not as if we're at each other's throats."

She didn't know how to explain the feeling that it was time to move out, to move on to her own life. "Dad…seriously, it's time. I just want to have my own place, to be responsible for myself. It has nothing to do with the house being too small. I just want to make decisions for myself, be on my own, pay my own way, walk through the door to something that's just mine. It's not that you'd never see me." She thought of the way her dad poked his nose in her business. At times, she wanted it as much as she didn't. "If you're trying to talk me out of it…"

He lifted his hand and shook his head. "I'm not talking you out of anything. I just wanted to touch base and understand. You know this doesn't mean you get to skip family night." He leaned back in the chair, resting his arm over the back of the empty one beside him. She understood what he was saying, and she didn't know why she wanted to be okay with it.

"I promise I'll be there," she said. The smile burst like a bright beam of sunshine in her stomach and pulled at her face, and her dad gestured to her.

"That there is something I want to see more of, that smile. And one more thing." He leaned across the table, looking to the side, and she held her breath a second, wondering what was coming next. "If your boss touches you like that again, that good ol' boy pat on the back, you tell him to keep his hands to himself, because if he doesn't, it'll be me who's in his face. Use your words and set your boundaries, or I will."

She didn't know what to say. Her dad was serious.

Every time Chad did that, she tried to tell herself that it was normal and shouldn't bother her like it did.

"Okay," she finally said.

He frowned. "Okay what? You'll speak up, or you want me to have a word with him? Because I will. You want me to fight your battles or teach you to fight?"

The answer was on the tip of her tongue as she dragged her gaze over to her boss, who strode out of the back with an apron around his waist, carrying three plates to a table. She knew how he looked at her and everyone else. Her boss was just one more asshole whose name was on her list.

"I'll tell him," she said. "But when he fires me, I'll tell him it was your idea."

Her dad laughed and shook his head. "Ah, Alison, Alison… That's my girl, jumping to the worst-case scenario. But, just FYI, he won't fire you. He can't, because if he does, it won't just be me he'll have to contend with—it'll be all the O'Connells, and I think you know well, darling daughter, that we look after our own. And one other thing: Just remember, when you move out, you can always move back home."

About the Author

"Lorhainne Eckhart is one of my go to authors when I want a guaranteed good book. So many twists and turns, but also so much love and such a strong sense of family."

(LORA W., REVIEWER)

New York Times & USA Today bestseller Lorhainne Eckhart is best known for writing Raw Relatable Real Romance where "Morals and family are running themes." As one fan calls her, she is the "Queen of the family saga." (aherman) writing "the ups and downs of what goes on within a family but also with some suspense, angst and of course a bit of romance thrown in for good measure." Follow Lorhainne on Bookbub to receive alerts on New Releases and Sales and join her mailing list at Lorhainne-Eckhart.com for her Monday Blog, all book news, give-aways and FREE reads. With over 120 books, audiobooks, and multiple series published and available at all, retailers now translated into six languages. She is a multiple recipient of the Readers' Favorite Award for Suspense and Romance, and lives in the Pacific Northwest on an island, is the mother of three, her oldest has autism and she is an advocate for never giving up on your dreams.

"Lorhainne Eckhart has this uncanny way of just hitting the spot every time with her books."

(CAROLINE L., REVIEWER)

The O'Connells: *The O'Connells of Livingston, Montana are not your typical family. A riveting collection of stories surrounding the ups and downs of what goes on within a family but also with some suspense, angst and of course a bit of romance thrown in for good measure. "I thought I loved the Friessens, but I absolutely adore the O'Connell's. Each and every book has different genres of stories, but the one thing in common is how she is able to wrap it around the family, which is the heart of each story." (C. Logue)*

The Friessens: *An emotional big family romance series, the Friessen family siblings find their relationships tested, lay their hearts on the line, and discover lasting love! "Lorhainne Eckhart is one of my go to authors when I want a guaranteed good book. So many twists and turns, but also so much love and such a strong sense of family." (Lora W., Reviewer)*

The Parker Sisters: *The Parker Sisters are a close-knit family, and like any other family they have their ups and downs. Eckhart has crafted another intense family drama… "The character development is outstanding, and the emotional investment is high…" (Aherman, Reviewer)*

The McCabe Brothers: *Join the five McCabe siblings on their journeys to the dark and dangerous side of love! An intense, exhilarating collection of romantic thrillers you won't want to miss. — "Eckhart has a new series that is definitely worth the read. The queen of the family saga started this series with a spin-off of her wildly successful Friessen series." From a Readers' Favorite award—winning author and "queen of the family saga" (Aherman)*

Billy Jo McCabe Mystery: *The social worker and the cop, an unlikely couple drawn together on a small, secluded Pacific Northwest island where nothing is as it seems. Protecting the innocent comes at a cost, and what seems to be a sleepy, quiet town is anything but.*

Lorhainne loves to hear from her readers! You can connect with me at:

www.LorhainneEckhart.com
lorhainneeckhart.le@gmail.com

facebook.com/AuthorLorhainneEckhart

twitter.com/LEckhart

instagram.com/lorhainneeckhart

bookbub.com/profile/lorhainne-eckhart

pinterest.com/lorhainneeckhart

In the Charm
Unexpected Consequences
It Was Always You
The First Time I Saw You
Welcome to My Arms
Welcome to Boston
I'll Always Love You
Ground Rules
A Reason to Breathe
You Are My Everything
Anything For You
The Homecoming
Stay Away From My Daughter
The Bad Boy
A Place of Our Own
The Visitor
All About Devon
Long Past Dawn
How to Heal a Heart
Keep Me In Your Heart

The O'Connells
The Neighbor
The Third Call
The Secret Husband
The Quiet Day
The Commitment
The Missing Father
The Hometown Hero
Justice
The Family Secret
The Fallen O'Connell
The Return of the O'Connells
And The She Was Gone

The Stalker
The O'Connell Family Christmas
The Girl Next Door
Broken Promises
The Gatekeeper
The Hunted

The Street Fighter
Finding Home

The McCabe Brothers
Don't Stop Me (Vic)
Don't Catch Me (Chase)
Don't Run From Me (Aaron)
Don't Hide From Me (Luc)
Don't Leave Me (Claudia)
Out of Time

A Billy Jo McCabe Mystery
Nothing As it Seems
Hiding in Plain Sight
The Cold Case
The Trap
Above the Law
The Stranger at the Door
The Children
The Last Stand
The Charity
The Sacrifice

The Wilde Brothers
The One (Joe and Margaret)
The Honeymoon, A Wilde Brothers Short
Friendly Fire (Logan and Julia)

Not Quite Married, A Wilde Brothers Short
A Matter of Trust (Ben and Carrie)
The Reckoning, A Wilde Brothers Christmas
Traded (Jake)
Unforgiven (Samuel)
The Holiday Bride

Married in Montana

His Promise
Love's Promise
A Promise of Forever

The Parker Sisters

Thrill of the Chase
The Dating Game
Play Hard to Get
What We Can't Have
Go Your Own Way
A June Wedding

Kate & Walker

One Night
Edge of Night
Last Night

Walk the Right Road Series

The Choice
Lost and Found
Merkaba
Bounty
Blown Away: The Final Chapter
He Came Back

The Saved Series

Saved
Vanished
Captured

Single Titles
Loving Christine